ROBERTS & MACLAY

Thriller

Copyright © 2021 by Roberts & Maclay (Roberts & Maclay Publishing). All rights reserved. No part of this book may be reproduced in any form or by any electronic or mechanical means, including information storage and retrieval systems, without written permission from the authors, except for the use of brief quotations in a book review.

Translator: Edwin Miles / Copyeditor: Philip Yaeger

Imprint: Independently published / ISBN: 9798715477293

Cover Art by reinhardfenzl.com

Cover Art was created with photos from:
depositphotos.com Nevakalina, sdecoret, orlaimagen, jag_cz, stevebonk, Dimedrol68, iLexx / shutterstock.com DR pics / and neo-stock.com

This is a work of fiction. Names, characters, businesses, places, events and incidents are either the products of the author's imagination or used in a fictitious manner. Any resemblance to actual persons, living or dead, or actual events is purely coincidental.

www.robertsmaclay.com

office@robertsmaclay.com

**Get the free Tom Wagner adventure
"The Stone of Destiny"**

— Learn more at the end of the book

"Only when there is nothing to hide can one maintain the greatest secrecy."

Chinese proverb

1

VIENNA AND BERLIN, 1976

The shrill scream of the telephone startled Arthur Julius Prey from sleep. He leaped out of bed and ran to the tiny office he kept in his Vienna apartment fast enough to stop it from ringing a second time. No need to wake his wife or daughter at this ungodly hour. As a freelance reporter, getting a call in the middle of the night did not necessarily mean the end of the world, but it usually didn't bode well. More often than not, a call like this would entail a long journey abroad and, to the chagrin of Wilhelmine and Maria, his wife and daughter, often to a crisis region steeped in danger.

He picked up the receiver and heard a young woman's voice say, "This is the long-distance operator in Berlin. You have a call from East Berlin. Please stay on the line."

East Berlin? He did not know anybody in Berlin, East or West. There was a buzz on the line, then a clicking sound.

"Arthur? Is that you?"

Arthur's eyes widened as he recognized his old friend's voice.

"Artjom! What is it? What are you doing in East Berlin?"

"Arthur, I need your help," the man said in his heavy Russian accent.

As he listened to what his friend had to say, a few framed photographs standing on the bookshelf beside his desk caught Arthur's eye. One showed himself and Artjom together. It had been taken on the most dangerous and terrifying mission of his career. With youthful exuberance, driven by a moral compass molded in the 1960s and inspired by Eddie Adams's Pulitzer Prize-winning photograph of the summary execution of a Vietcong prisoner by a South Vietnamese police chief in February 1968, Arthur had joined the Associated Press—and just six months later found himself smack in the middle of the Vietnam War.

After slogging through weeks of hardship and misery, Arthur had witnessed a bombing raid while on a day's R&R in Saigon. He had gone to the aid of a young girl hurt in a blast but had been taken by surprise by another explosion and was injured himself. Father Lazarev had given him first aid and saved the lives of both Arthur and the young girl. He had not moved from their bedsides in the hospital. An experience like that forges a bond, and they had been close friends ever since.

A year earlier, Arthur had finally found the time to visit the man who had saved his life. Through contacts, he had managed to travel to the Soviet Union and, more importantly, to get out again safely. While there, he had spent a few weeks in a small village east of Moscow. There, in a crumbling wooden church beside a small lake, the second photo that held a place of honor on Arthur's bookshelf had been taken.

Twenty-four hours after the call from his friend, Arthur found himself walking along Friedrichstrasse in Berlin. He stopped to look at the Berlin Wall and the famous square in front of it, with its white wooden hut: Checkpoint Charlie. Just behind the hut began the narrow no-man's-land that separated East and West. Since 1961, gray cement, barbed wire and armored vehicles had tainted the day-to-day views confronting Berlin's inhabitants. The windows of the buildings that stood alongside the wall were all bricked up, but graffiti added a little color to the bleakness, at least on the western side. Many refugees seeking freedom beyond the walls had died in that bordering strip of land. Those who tried to flee from East to West were shot without mercy.

Arthur looked at the time, turned away and went down the next narrow side street. He had to be at the meeting point on time.

It was late, and the streets around the border crossing were deserted. Arthur strode quickly down the alley before turning again. They had arranged to meet at the next intersection. Eleven p.m. on the dot, not one minute later, his friend had said. He looked at his watch: 10:54. He was alone. The air was cold and damp, and he felt a chill creeping into his bones. An uneasy feeling slowly grew in his belly. On the opposite side of the dimly lit street, a drunk staggered out of a bar and swayed along the sidewalk. Arthur paced anxiously. The few minutes felt like an eternity. Then an old VW T1 microbus turned slowly around a corner and rolled toward him. Arthur looked in from the passenger side when the van rolled to a stop.

"Get in the back. Come on, quick," hissed the man at the wheel, looking around nervously.

Arthur hesitated, but did as he was told. He looked around, opened the rear door and climbed into the windowless microbus. Hardly had he sat down when the man turned around and held out a black cloth sack.

"Put this on," the man said. Surprised, Arthur took the sack. *What have I gotten myself into here?* he wondered as he pulled the sack over his head. The driver hit the gas.

2

CHURCH OF OUR LADY OF KAZAN, LAKE SVETLOYAR,
NEAR NIZHNY NOVGOROD, RUSSIA. PRESENT DAY.

Two men scouted the grounds around the church, before finally approaching it from different directions. They took up posts at the entrance of the church, in the pale light of the moon.

Lake Svetloyar looked small, but it was far deeper than one would expect from its size. The moon shone brightly, reflected in the calm surface of the lake. The church, built entirely of wood, had stood on the shore of the lake for almost a century, and in the silvery glow of the moonlight it looked almost unnaturally mystical.

The two guards seemed bored, but they were professional enough to take their jobs seriously. The clothes they wore seemed inherently unsuited to their surroundings: they were dressed in suits, specially tailored to conceal the contours that pistols and shoulder holsters usually made. Only one paved road led to and from the church, connecting it to the Voskresensky district. Reaching the church meant crossing an old, ramshackle-looking bridge. A third guard had been posted there.

As he did every evening, the priest knelt before the altar of the small church and thanked God for choosing him. He thought of the many guardians before him who had dedicated their lives to preserving the secret—a secret that indeed meant little to most of the world outside, but meant everything to the people there. Only a few knew the legend, and even fewer knew about the treasures, both material and spiritual, that he had dedicated his life to protecting—as many before him had done.

The breeze whistled lightly through the cracks in the wooden walls of the church. There was never a moment of absolute silence here. Something was always creaking or cracking or squeaking somewhere, so the priest did not look up when he heard noises from outside, in front of the entrance. It was probably one of the brown bears that frequented the area and which he saw almost daily, he thought. But he knew that he was safe inside the church. The guards had been hired on the advice of his son.

The priest was starting to think that his time was growing short. He was approaching his eighty-fifth birthday, and God alone knew how much longer he would be among the living. He felt healthy and energetic, but he knew that could change very quickly at his age. He would make the preparations he needed to make. A successor needed to be found as soon as possible.

Outside, four men in camouflage appeared, as if from nowhere. Equipped with night vision equipment and with MP5 submachine guns at the ready, they crept quietly toward the church, doing their best to conceal themselves in the shadows cast by the bright moon. One of the guards saw them instantly, but was too slow. He had no time either to shoot or sound an alarm. A bullet between the eyes and he was dead before his body hit the ground.

As the other guard turned to see what had happened, he too was eliminated.

The coast was clear.

3

HEADQUARTERS OF BLUE SHIELD TASK FORCE, UNO CITY, VIENNA

Tom, Hellen and Cloutard flipped open the files that the woman now in charge of Blue Shield had just handed them. Almost simultaneously, their eyes widened and their jaws dropped. Absolute silence fell for several seconds.

Tom was the first to recover. "Is this what I think it is?"

Theresia de Mey, Hellen's mother and the new head of Blue Shield, nodded, unable to suppress a smile.

"*Mon Dieu*, so it is not just a myth. It truly exists?" Cloutard asked.

Hellen's mother nodded again.

"And we get to go find it?" Tom asked. Impressed, he turned down the corners of his mouth and narrowed his eyes in his best Robert de Niro imitation. "No dime-a-dozen artifacts for us."

Hellen had not yet said a word. She went on studying the file, poring over the attached maps and analyzing the photographs in the appendix. She had to press one hand over her mouth to physically stop herself from letting out a joyful whoop. She looked up at Tom and Cloutard.

"You know what this means? People have been hunting for this for centuries. It's one of the greatest legends of human history."

"And we finally have conclusive evidence of exactly where it is," said Theresia de Mey proudly. "Now all you need to do is find it for Blue Shield."

Tom rubbed his hands together enthusiastically. "I'm ready to go any time. On the hunt for—"

The ringing of Tom's cell phone interrupted his euphoria, and his expression instantly cycled from astonishment, through doubt, to concern.

"The Vatican," he said, and took the call.

Hellen and Cloutard looked on expectantly, but Hellen's mother seemed suddenly peeved. Cloutard saw her pinched lips and quickly tried to placate her: "It is only the Pope. We should be happy that Tom was not in the, uh, men's room when His Holiness decided to call."

Hellen's mother looked at the Frenchman in astonishment. She did not understand what was happening at all. Tom, in the meantime, had hung up and had risen to his feet.

"The Pope needs a favor. He's expecting the Patriarch of the Russian Orthodox Church very soon for an ecumenical powwow, and they've had a series of terror and bomb threats. He wants me to work with the Swiss Guard to guarantee their safety." He pointed at the file with the Blue Shield job. "That's going to have to wait for now."

Hellen drew a sharp breath. "Wait? You want us to wait? Tom, this is one of humanity's greatest treasures, lost for centuries, and we're supposed to *wait*?"

"Do I have to remind you that His Holiness was extremely helpful during our last little escapade? And what about the secret he revealed to you? I owe—no, *we* owe him for that."

Theresia de Mey sniffed angrily.

"Mr. Wagner—" she began, but cut herself off because she had not said his name correctly. She had pronounced it as if it were German—"Vahgner"—but now corrected herself and stretched the "a" for emphasis. "Mr. Waaaagner. We don't want to wait any longer. We cannot. You can't seriously think it's a good idea to put THIS job on hold and make me and Blue Shield wait on your first day on the job?"

But Tom didn't even hear the last half of her speech. He had already left the conference room.

"*Ma chère*," said François Cloutard, giving Hellen's mother with his best big-eyed puppy-dog look. "*Ce n'est pas un problème*. It has not been found in all this time, hundreds of years. A few days more or less will make no difference."

The de Meys, both mother and daughter, were speechless.

"*Croyez-moi*, for myself, as a former grave robber and art smuggler, this is also very hard to accept, but without Tom the mission will simply have to wait."

He stood up, straightened his tie and put on his hat. Hellen also started gathering her things to leave. Cloutard was right. As much as she hated the thought, they had to wait until Tom returned.

Cloutard stopped in the doorway and turned back to Theresia de Mey once more.

"And would you be so kind as to make sure the coffee is better next time? We are in Vienna, *pour l'amour de Dieu*."

4

CHURCH OF OUR LADY OF KAZAN, LAKE SVETLOYAR.

The silence was suddenly shattered by a loud crash. The old priest started and looked around in shock. He was no longer young, and it took him a few seconds to get from his knees to his feet. He turned around only to find himself staring down the barrels of three machine pistols with laser sights. Three men in battle gear had just kicked open the door and forced their way into his inner sanctum. Three red beams were trained on him. His breath and heart stood still. One of the three approached while the other two kept their weapons aimed at him.

"I don't want to spill any more blood. You know something that we need to know. And you will tell us."

The man spoke Russian with no accent whatsoever, flawless and polished. He spoke so perfectly, in fact, that he could not possibly be Russian. The priest guessed that he was German, but that was only one of countless thoughts that shot through his mind as the man snapped handcuffs on his wrists. He had opened the visor of his helmet and the priest looked up into cold gray eyes. But he saw something strange, too. The man had neither eyelashes nor eyebrows, and the priest suspected that he didn't have a hair on his entire body—another thought that, considering his situation, was completely out of place. It was also the last thing that went through his mind before the intruder jabbed a thin needle into the crook of his arm. Seconds later, the priest passed out.

A moment later, a fourth man entered the church. He ignored the two dead guards and the unconscious priest lying on the floor and instead went straight to the altar. He opened the wooden tabernacle that hung on the wall behind it and slid the back wall aside with practiced ease, revealing an ornate and exceptionally valuable cross that lay hidden in a hollow space behind it. The man removed it from the tabernacle and stowed it in a small leather bag.

"Let's send this on a little trip so it can finally do what it's meant to."

Two of the men lifted the unconscious priest between them.

"Are you sure you want let the cross out of your hands?"

"Don't worry. It will find its way back again soon enough."

The men left the church and laid the priest inside a brand-new white delivery van. The man with the cross in the bag closed the church door and climbed into the van as well. Gravel crunched beneath the tires as the driver tapped the gas and drove away.

5

WEST BERLIN, 1976

Although he had spent the drive trying to concentrate on when the VW turned and how long it seemed to travel straight, Arthur had no idea where he was. But he felt certain he was still in West Berlin. When the microbus finally pulled to a stop in a dark courtyard, the driver pulled him from back and led him a few steps down into a cellar. They passed through seemingly endless passages until finally the man pressed Arthur down onto a chair. The room felt clammy and stank of mold. Water dripped ceaselessly from the ceiling.

What had his friend dragged him into? Arthur wondered. Was he a spy after all, as Arthur had always suspected?

Berlin was a Cold War hotspot. People, goods and information were smuggled across the border in the most creative ways. For some, it meant a lucrative trade, despite the danger. Many in the East saw Coca-Cola as a symbol of freedom, but was it worth putting your life on the line for?

"Can I take this stinking sack off my head?" Arthur asked when he finally heard steps approaching, then whispering.

"Yes, you can," Arthur heard, and he recognized the voice of his friend.

He peeled the sack off with relief, stood up and dropped it on the chair. Artjom was standing in front of him with his arms spread wide in greeting. Somewhat bewildered by this effusive welcome, Arthur threw his arms around his friend and at the same time looked around inside the gloomy room. After their call, Arthur had feared the worst.

Artjom Lazarev—or better, Father Artjom Lazarev—was a Russian Orthodox priest. And as Arthur had always feared, he was also apparently a spy.

After the Second World War, the orthodox church had found itself under strict state control, which led to its being infiltrated by the KGB and others. Clerics were forced to serve as informants, sometimes even as agents. Back then, Father Lazarev had made use of his state and KGB contacts and had had himself smuggled into Vietnam to help the poorest of the poor and, presumably, to do a little spying. Everything had its price.

"What's going on? Where are we?" Arthur asked.

Father Lazarev indicated for him to wait a moment and went across to the man who had picked Arthur up on the street. He whispered into his ear and the man immediately left the two of them alone in the room.

"This is a secret passage between East and West. A smuggling route. A group of young Easterners built it and managed to help more than fifty people get through it to freedom."

Father Lazarev swung his arm around Arthur's shoulders and led him around the cellar. In the next room, Arthur saw a hole about three feet across in the center of the floor. A wooden framework with a winch had been erected above it.

"From here it goes forty feet straight down. Then you have to crawl through a tunnel for a hundred yards." Arthur eyed his friend. That explained his outfit: an old pair of overalls, smeared with mud from shoulder to foot. It was an unaccustomed sight for Arthur, who was more familiar with Artjom in his traditional black robes.

"Why am I here? Why all the secrecy? You said you needed my help." Arthur stared down into the hole in amazement. "So how can I help you?"

"It is so good to see you again." Father Lazarev beamed at Arthur, then grasped him by both shoulders and shook him a little. "Come, my friend. Come!"

Arthur followed him into another room. On a rickety folding table stood a small but artfully worked wooden casket. Strangely, though, it appeared to be completely seamless, with no visible lid or lock. And it looked ancient. Father Lazarev picked it up and handed it to Arthur.

"I want you to look after this for me. Get it as far away from here as possible and hide it where nobody will be able to find it."

Arthur was perplexed. He had been running through all kinds of scenarios, but this had not been one of them.

"What is it?" he asked, looking at the box from all sides.

"Please do me this favor. It is a matter of utmost importance." He laid his hands on Arthur's, which were wrapped tightly around the box. "It is safer if you know as little as possible about it. I hope that I will one day be able to protect the case myself, but until that day look after it well."

"But—"

"I'm sorry to have to play this card, but . . . I believe you are still in my debt. Or do I have that wrong?" He smiled at Arthur.

With resignation, Arthur smiled back. He nodded.

"Now let us have a drink to the old days."

From a linen bag, Father Lazarev produced a bottle of Russian vodka and two glasses, and poured them full. They raised their glasses.

"*Twajó sdarówje!*"

6

FIUMICINO AIRPORT, ROME

The customs officer looked up in surprise at the man who had just handed him his passport: he was completely bald. More than bald, in fact. Hairless. Not a hair on his head, no beard, no eyebrows, no eyelashes.

Madonna . . . the customs man thought. Day in, day out, he processed the most absurd spectrum of humankind. Oddballs and characters, drop-dead gorgeous women, indescribably ugly men, and everything in between. But an utterly hairless individual was a first, even for him. He had to make an effort not to stare at the man longer than absolutely necessary.

"*Benvenuto a Roma,*" he said as he handed the passport back.

The man's expression did not change as he headed toward the exit. He left the baggage carousel to the left and passed through the automatic doors into the arrivals hall. It was the usual scene: people waiting expectantly for their loved ones, waving bouquets of flowers and holding banners that said "*Benvenuto*," children running around, couples kissing, bored taxi and limousine drivers waiting with placards scrawled with unpronounceable names.

He looked for the sign that read "Mr. Smith." He was not in a good mood, and hated when plans changed. He detested having to improvise—too many imponderables, too many short-term variables over which he had no influence. The demands he placed on himself would normally have stopped him from accepting a job like this. But the pay was far too attractive. And the client was not someone you could simply turn down.

The "driver" spotted him first and waved him over. Without a word of greeting, the hairless man, known professionally as the Kahle, followed him to the garage. When they reached an Alfa Romeo Stevio Quadrifoglio, the driver stopped and looked around. The garage was empty, and the car was parked beyond the range of the numerous security cameras. The man opened the trunk and drew a blanket aside. Looking inside, the Kahle found a backpack. He opened it to reveal a brand-new, dismantled G22A2 sniper rifle with a 25X riflescope, bipod, ammunition, a digital ballistic calculator and wind sensors, all laid out neatly in corresponding foam cutouts. He briefly checked the equipment and nodded, satisfied. Before closing the backpack again, he surreptitiously slipped the SOG Fusion Salute Black tactical knife from one of the rubber loops.

"Configured exactly to your specifications," the driver said, and handed him the car key.

"*Grazie per l'aiuto*," said the Kahle in perfect Italian, and a moment later stabbed the man expertly in the ear. Not a sound, no blood. His eyes rolled upward and he collapsed. The Kahle heaved the limp body into the back of the Alfa, pulled the trunk closed and drove away.

7

OFFICE OF THE SWISS GUARD, VATICAN CITY, ROME

"You're late, Wagner." Lorenzo Da Silva sounded peeved.

"How can I be late, Commander? I've literally just flown in." Tom grinned as he held out his hand in greeting, but Da Silva ignored the gesture.

Although they had never met, the commandant of the Swiss Guard could not abide Tom, and for one simple reason: Da Silva looked at Tom as a foreign body, nothing more. Tom was not Swiss and he had never trained as a Swiss guard. And because of that, he represented a break in a tradition that had stood the test of centuries. Da Silva would never question the word of the Holy Father, or even think about criticizing him, but for the life of him he could not understand what the Pope saw in this guy.

"Every man is at his post. They all know what to do. But you could not even get here in time for the briefing." Da Silva practically spat the words at Tom.

"Take it easy, Lorenzo. I've been briefed by the very top. The Pope himself has told me all I need to know. He also put me in touch briefly with the head of the Patriarch's security detail. I'm up to speed and ready to go. So where are our peas-in-the-pod now?"

"Peas-in-the-pod?" Da Silva asked, his tone even icier than before. The fact that the Pope had gone over his own head and called Wagner personally was an affront that heated his otherwise cool and calculating Swiss constitution to the boiling point. *He was the commandant of the Swiss Guard, godda—* Da Silva almost cursed inwardly, but he caught himself in time.

"The two P's! P & P. Pope and Patriarch." Tom gave the Swiss guardsman a crooked grin.

Da Silva rolled his eyes. "Kyrill II, Patriarch of the Russian Orthodox Church, has come from Russia to discuss a number of important ecumenical matters with the Pope. Afterward, they will celebrate an ecumenical mass together. Given the terrorist threats we've received, we are at the highest level of alert."

Tom nodded. He took life as casually as he could most of the time and had no problem at all putting himself in harm's way, but he was also a professional and he knew when it was time to stop messing around. He had a job to do. Without waiting for Da Silva, he strode off in the direction of the Pope's chambers.

Pope Sixtus VI smiled when he saw Tom, who immediately knelt and kissed the Ring of the Fisherman on the Pope's hand. Etiquette aside, the Pope patted him warmly on the shoulder. "I hope Da Silva did not come down on you too hard. He is a good man, although his ego tends to get in his way sometimes. But who are we to judge?"

The Pope shook his head vigorously and a smile flashed on his face. Tom smiled too. He liked this wise old man very much. And how Da Silva treated him was a walk in the park compared to Colonel Maierhofer, his former commander in the Austrian elite unit Cobra.

Together, they left the Pope's chambers on the third floor and went down to the floor below. There, in the Seconda Loggia of the Apostolic Palace, the Pope received the Patriarch and his entourage.

8

VATICAN CITY, ROME

When the mass and the subsequent media scrum were over, the Pope took Tom aside. "This is the Patriarch's first visit to the Holy City. It would please me very much to show him something of the Vatican. I know that deviates a little from the day's agenda, but it is important to me. Can you manage that?"

"Of course, Your Holiness."

Tom saw no security issues within the walls of the Vatican, and so far the day had passed quietly enough. There had not been so much as a whiff of any kind of incident. But even though the terror warnings had apparently turned out to be false and a raised alert level was still in place at every entrance to the Holy City, Tom was not about to take his responsibility lightly. He insisted on remaining with the group, very much to the displeasure of Lorenzo Da Silva.

"Your Holiness—" the guardsman began to protest.

"Thank you for your patience and understanding, Commandant Da Silva. God will thank you for it." The Pope laid a hand gently on Da Silva's shoulder, and the commandant lowered his head reverently.

"My thanks, Your Holiness."

Tom turned to Da Silva and gave him a friendly jab in the side.

"See? We can all be friends here. Come on."

The Pope went first, leading the group through the Sistine Chapel and the Vatican gardens and onward to the library. Tom smiled to himself, knowing that a few very interesting parts of the library were not included in the tour. He was well aware of how great an honor Hellen, Cloutard and he himself had been accorded—not long ago, they had been able to visit the most secret section of the archive in person.

At the end of the tour, the Pope wanted to pay a visit to the Tomb of St. Peter, which held special significance for Tom.

Swiss Guardsmen were posted along the entire route. There was not a tourist in sight. Tom could easily imagine what that would mean. Right this minute, there were presumably hundreds of visitors to Rome standing at closed entrances, and no doubt the poor Vatican employees were suffering some strongly worded protests. Tom felt his own excitement grow as they descended into the Vatican Necropolis. At the front of the group were the Pope and Patriarch, the two men chatting away animatedly. One did not get an impression at all that they were the two highest church officials in the world; they seemed more like two old friends with a lot to catch up on. Deep in conversation, they took little notice of the centuries-old history all around them.

"Ah, and here we are at last," said the Pope when they reached St. Peter's Tomb. He was just starting to say something about the gravesite and the crypt when he suddenly paused. He pointed to an object that lay atop the tomb. "What is that? What is it doing here?" he asked in surprise.

9

ST. PETER'S TOMB, VATICAN CITY, ROME

Lorenzo and Tom looked at each other in surprise, then both moved to the tomb. Directly beside the Sword of Peter, with which Tom was already all too familiar, was an object that had no right to be where it lay. Tom picked up the elaborate-looking object and examined it.

A strange sensation suddenly came over him. He felt as if he had seen the artifact somewhere before. There was something extremely familiar about it, but Tom's thoughts were rudely interrupted by Da Silva.

"Wagner!" he barked, snapping Tom back to the moment. Hesitantly, Tom handed the object to the Pope, much to Da Silva's annoyance. *It should have been examined first*, the guardsman thought. *For fingerprints, explosives, contact poison . . .* just three of the things that immediately sprang to Da Silva's mind as he glared disdainfully at Tom.

Tom's gut feeling was telling him that what they had just found was the start of something much bigger. Why else would someone go to this trouble and put themselves at so much risk, if not for something terribly important? The Pope and the Patriarch stared at the object in the Pope's hands—an exceptionally ornate, gold orthodox cross. The Patriarch and those with him looked at each other in surprise.

It's old. Ancient, even, Tom realized, then smiled to himself as he thought: *Hellen's never around when you need her*.

"How did this get here?" Da Silva snarled at the two guardsmen posted at the entrance to the crypt. They were supposed to have checked the entire area for anything unusual or dangerous before the Pope entered.

One of the guardsmen stepped forward. He seemed honestly surprised. "It wasn't there when I checked the crypt, sir."

Da Silva snapped into crisis mode. He took the cross from the Pope's hand. "Your Holiness, we have to have forensics examine the cross. The security of the entire city is in jeopardy if foreign objects start appearing from nowhere in this holy place."

"A foreign object? That is a *cross*, Commandant Da Silva." The Pope's voice suddenly carried a note of warning. Da Silva instinctively lowered his head and excused himself.

"Your Holiness," Tom said, "we could consult with Hellen. If this cross has any historical significance, she will recognize it," he suggested.

"We have enough experts in the Vatican. I don't think we need to drag in another outsider," Commandant Da Silva said with a sniff. Wagner was trying to bypass him once again. But the Pope narrowed his eyes coldly at Da Silva, and the guardsman dared not say another word.

"Hellen will know at a glance what it is," Tom went on.

The Pope ignored the evil eye Da Silva was giving Tom. He nodded thoughtfully. "Let's do it your way," he said.

10

OFFICE OF THE POPE, VATICAN CITY, ROME

When everyone had returned to the Apostolic Palace, Tom flipped open his MacBook and started a video call. He held the cross in front of the camera.

"Whoa!" Hellen cried. "This is . . . this is incredible."

"What's incredible?" said Tom, asking aloud what everyone in the room was thinking. The Pope, the Patriarch, the camerlengo and the Patriarch's party were bursting with curiosity. Even Sister Lucrezia, who had just served tea to everyone and greeted Tom with her usual effusiveness, had stayed.

"If it were not absurd and impossible, then I'd say that what you're holding looks like"—she took a deep breath —"the Cross of Kitezh!"

When the Patriarch heard Hellen's words, he almost fell out of his chair in shock. He paled visibly as he looked wide-eyed at his secretary, Father Fjodor. "The Cross of Kitezh," the Patriarch whispered, his voice trembling.

"The cross of what?" Tom asked, still struggling to work out why the cross seemed so familiar to him.

"It's a long story. I'll have to see it myself," Hellen said. If it were humanly possible, she would have reached straight through the screen, Tom could tell.

"Hellen, please don't let me die ignorant," Tom said impatiently. "Who's Kitezh?"

"Kitezh is not a *who*, Tom. The question should be: What is Kitezh?" Hellen looked at Tom with a smile, and he knew that she had tasted blood.

11

MAKLI NECROPOLIS, PAKISTAN

Berlin Brice, better known as the Welshman, sat in a CJ-5 Jeep that was almost as ancient as he was and directed his men as they loaded crates of looted goods onto trucks. The Makli Necropolis, one of the largest graveyards in the world, covers an area of twenty-five acres close to the city of Thatta in Sindh province, Pakistan. There are somewhere between half a million and a million graves at the site, dating from the 14th to the 18th century. Although the graveyard was declared a UNESCO World Heritage site as far back as the 1980s, the area has still not been properly researched—for organized grave robbers, a rich feeding ground.

"Be careful with those, damn you! They aren't vegetable crates," the Welshman swore in Urdu, but it had little effect on the men working. The sun beat down mercilessly, a hundred and twenty degrees in the shade, and there were still countless crates to load. The Welshman rolled his eyes. His satellite phone rang.

"Qadir, please make it very clear to these bastards that they will not get a single rupee from me if they continue to handle my finds like that."

Qadir nodded, raised his AK-47 and rattled off several shots into the air. Then he bellowed at the men in a voice that would have put the fear of God into a U.S. Marine drill sergeant. The men nodded submissively.

"Well," the old man said to himself, "would you look at that." He picked up the Thuraya X5-Touch and answered the call.

"We've found it, sir."

The Welshman leaned back and let out a sigh of relief. Suddenly, all the plundered goods he'd accumulated here so far were just pocket change. Everything paled in comparison to the treasure he was now one step closer to.

"The entrance?"

"No sir, not the entrance. But we know who has the casket."

The Welshman grunted and was on the verge of an angry reply when a shot made him jump. He looked back over his shoulder. Qadir had just shot one of the workers dead: the man had apparently managed to drop one of the crates. The other workers stared aghast at Qadir and began loading twice as fast.

The Welshman shrugged. "One less man to pay. I like it when my employees show initiative to save me money."

"Pardon?" said the voice on the phone, confused.

"Not you, idiot. Stop beating around the bush, this isn't some damned quiz show. What have you found?"

"We were able to trace back the casket's trail. We now know when and to whom the guardian passed it on."

The man paused. The Welshman was growing impatient. "This isn't some who-fucking-dunit! Give me a name!"

"You won't believe this, but he's related to the grandfather of someone we know quite well: Tom Wagner."

The Welshman smiled. Wherever Wagner was, Cloutard would not be far away. And he had unfinished business with both of them. He had to stop them from throwing a wrench in the works again.

"Good. Get the casket and get rid of Wagner's old grandpa."

"The connection's bad, Sir. What was that about a Wagner opera?" the caller asked, puzzled.

The Welshman blew his stack. "Remind me to smash your face in the next time we meet. Now listen carefully: I want you to kill Tom Wagner's grandfather. Shoot him, strangle him, blow him up, drown him, quarter him, whatever takes your fancy. Just get rid of him. And then bring me the fucking box!"

12

POPE'S CHAMBERS, VATICAN CITY, ROME

"Kitezh is a sunken city. Or rather, it's the legend surrounding a sunken city. It's sometimes called the Russian Atlantis—according to the myth, it's supposed to have vanished beneath the waters of Lake Svetloyar in Russia, not far from Nizhny Novgorod," Hellen said.

"People have looked for the sunken city for centuries, treasure hunters and archeologists especially," the Russian Patriarch said, his voice lowered to a reverent whisper. "In recent years they've even scoured the lake floor with diving equipment. If this really is the Cross of Kitezh, it would be an unparalleled sensation for Russia."

The Pope laid one hand soothingly on the old Patriarch's shoulder. He looked at Tom, tilted his head a little to one side, and with unmistakable irony said, "Yet another adventure, Tom?"

Tom grimaced apologetically and raised his hands as if to say it was all just pure coincidence.

"Where did the cross come from if the city is underwater?" Tom asked, looking into the laptop's camera to direct the question at Hellen.

"That's the million-dollar question, isn't it? And unfortunately we have no way to know the answer," Hellen said with some resignation. "Until a few minutes ago, I'd always considered Kitezh to be a fairy story. Like many of my staid colleagues, I never even dreamed that the legend might hold a grain of truth."

"I'm more interested in finding out how the cross came to be lying on top of the Tomb of St. Peter," Commandant Da Silva interrupted. "It's one thing for an object of historical value to turn up, but someone has managed to gain unauthorized access to the Vatican and the Necropolis, and that has to be our top priority." Da Silva's harsh voice cut through the air like a chainsaw.

"Truly, it is more important for us to know where the cross came from," the Patriarch said. "The Cross of Kitezh is one of the most crucial artifacts of the 'invisible city,' as we Russians like to call it."

"And the mere fact that the cross exists means there is a chance of finding the city itself," Father Fjodor added excitedly.

Hellen, too, was thrilled at the find and impatient to know more. "That's true," she said. "If Kitezh still exists, then there must be a reason that someone deposited the cross in the Necropolis. And that must be someone who knows where Kitezh is. At least, I hope so."

"But why would someone suddenly steer all our attention toward a legend that no one really seems to think is true and that no one is looking for? And more importantly, why now, with a delegation from Russia visiting? That's what we really need to find out," Tom said, glancing across at the Pope.

13

POPE'S CHAMBERS, VATICAN CITY, ROME

Da Silva was shaking his head. "*You* don't get to find out anything, Wagner. You're in the Vatican as a guest, and if anyone's going to open an investigation here, it's me. The first question is, for whom was this strange message meant?"

"Could it have been intended for Your Holiness?" Father Fjodor, the Patriarch's secretary, piped up.

The Patriarch looked at his companion in surprise, but then nodded benevolently. "The Cross of Kitezh is one of our oldest legends. As Mr. Wagner mentioned, maybe whoever left it there knew that we would be here and would visit the tomb, and they used it to get our attention."

"Impossible!" Da Silva interjected. "No one knew about the tour through the Vatican in advance, let alone where we would actually go. I'd stake my honor—my life!—on it."

The Patriarch was unmoved by Da Silva's outburst. "The question is, what can we do?" he said.

All eyes turned expectantly to the Pope.

"With all due respect, Your Holiness," said Tom, his voice uncharacteristically subdued, "I would like very much to speak with you alone."

Without waiting for the Pope's reply, the Patriarch excused himself and left the room. His secretary followed silently. Da Silva and Sister Lucrezia gritted their teeth, but at a nod from the Pope they also departed.

"Alone but with Hellen, you mean," said the Pope, indicating the screen of Tom's laptop, where Hellen's face still showed.

Tom nodded. "Since the first moment I saw the cross, I've had the feeling that I'd seen it before," he said.

"Why does that not surprise me?" said the Pope, with just a trace of sarcasm.

Hellen seemed puzzled. "I thought you'd never heard of Kitezh?"

"I haven't. But I *have* seen that cross. All this time, I've been trying to think where it was, and now I've managed to dredge up the memory. My grandfather once showed me a picture of himself and one of his oldest friends. The man was a Russian Orthodox priest from Nizhny Novgorod, and in the photograph he was holding this cross in his hands." Tom smiled mischievously. It was certainly not the first time he'd managed to surprise Hellen, but the astonished look on the Pope's face was priceless.

"What do you suggest, Tom? You've seen how important Kitezh is for the Patriarch. He would appreciate it very much if you were able to find his invisible city. One thing is clear to me: this is a sign from the Almighty." The Pope was suddenly on his feet and there was veneration in his voice—Tom had heard it once before, back in the crypt beneath the Sagrada Familia: "It is no coincidence that you both are here," he said.

Hellen was grinning from ear to ear.

"Okay, here's a plan," Tom said. "Hellen, you and Cloutard pay a visit to my grandfather and see what information you can get out of him. We have to find out all we can about the cross and who his friend in the photo is. I'll fly straight to Russia tomorrow. Maybe I can fly with the Patriarch?" Tom looked up at the Pope and smiled enquiringly. "Once you've talked to Pop, you fly to Nizhny Novgorod. I'll meet you and Cloutard there tomorrow night. It seems like the logical place to start looking."

Hellen nodded and beamed at Tom on the screen. "Searching for Kitezh is just as exciting as the job Blue Shield just gave us."

"If you say so," Tom said, returning her grin. The Pope and Tom said goodbye to Hellen and the screen went dark.

"May God protect you," said the Holy Father and crossed himself. "Be careful."

14

VATICAN CITY, ROME

"What a restaurant looks like is irrelevant, *mon ami*. In Rome, you can tell a good *trattoria* by how many locals are sitting inside."

There were few things that mattered as much to François Cloutard as good food and the right bottle of wine, except perhaps antique artifacts and stolen works of art. And now that Tom had called him after his talk with the Pope, Cloutard was more than happy to share his Rome restaurant tips with Tom.

"François, I won't be flying to Nizhny Novgorod until tomorrow morning, so I'll be spending the night here in Rome. Do you know a good pizzeria?"

"*Mon Dieu*, a pizzeria? You are a philistine, Tom, the dictionary definition of a philistine. Italians do not go to pizzerias to eat. In a traditional Italian restaurant, they do not even serve pizza. They serve real Italian food."

A diatribe followed about antipasti, pasta, *frutti di mare* and other Italian delicacies, few of which Tom could even pronounce. After a good five minutes, Tom finally managed to interrupt Cloutard.

"All right, all right! Can't you just send me the address of a restaurant you can recommend?"

"*Naturellement*," the Frenchman said, as if his honor had been wounded. "*Ecoute,* Tom*, la chose la plus importante est*: you are not to eat before 9 pm. A person who sets foot in a restaurant before that will be instantly stamped as an ignorant tourist and will end up with whatever leftovers they have from the day before."

"Ah. Okay. I did not know that. Good tip."

"So here is my recommendation: you go to a restaurant called Cacio e Pepe and you order their namesake dish, *cacio e pepe*, as an appetizer, followed by *orecchiette pesto pachino pinoli*. As a *secondi*, order the *straccetti di manzo al rosmarino*, then *ricotta e cioccolato* for *dolci*.

"François, do you really keep the menus of every good European restaurant in your head?"

"Of course not. What an absurd notion. I also know the menus of the best North African, Arabian and South American establishments, of course. The rest of the world, if you ask me, is unpalatable."

A few seconds later, Tom's phone pinged with a text message: the address of Cacio e Pepe. Cloutard knew perfectly well that Tom would have trouble remembering spaghetti bolognese at the moment, partly because his mind was somewhere else completely.

He could not stop thinking about the cross—in fact, it had even distracted his attention from the rumored terrorist threat. What did his grandfather have to do with the Cross of Kitezh? Why was the cross lying on the Tomb of St. Peter? How did it even get there? All these questions were spinning through his head as he left the Holy City and strolled past the cylindrical edifice of Castel Sant'Angelo, following the Tiber upstream. He was so deep in thought that he did not notice the bald man who began to follow him at St. Peter's Square. The man wore a fairly large backpack, but that was not unusual for a tourist. He followed Tom until he turned left at the Ponte Matteotti and entered a *trattoria* not far from Piazza Mazzini.

An hour and a half later, the man was still standing outside the restaurant. As usual in Rome, even at this late hour the streets were still filled with people, and he stopped a young boy, about ten years old, on the street.

"How'd you like earn ten euros?" the man asked, coloring his flawless Italian with a dose of rough Roman dialect.

The boy's eyes gleamed and he nodded eagerly. "*Si, Signore.*"

The man handed the boy a ten-euro note and an envelope. He pointed across the street. "There's a guy sitting over there in Cacio e Pepe." He showed the boy his phone. On the display was a picture of Tom. "Take this envelope to him, but don't tell him who gave it to you. He's an old friend of mine and I've got a big surprise for him, so you can't tell him anything about it, okay?"

The boy nodded. He snatched the envelope and the ten euros and ran across the road. The Kahle smiled and glanced at his watch. He still had a good hour. He turned and headed back toward the Tiber, crossed the river at Ponte Regina Margherita and continued on, moving southeast.

Meanwhile, the boy had entered the overflowing restaurant. It was loud and stuffy, waiters scooted among the tables, and people sang and laughed and raised their glasses in toasts—a typical evening in a typical Roman restaurant. The boy scanned the tables until he saw Tom sitting alone at a table in a back corner, picking at his pasta and lost in thought. The boy recognized him immediately. He went and laid the envelope on the table and, before Tom had really taken any notice of him, had already vanished again out the door.

Tom frowned. He picked up the envelope cautiously by one edge and held it up to the light. It looked like a normal letter, but an uneasy feeling came over him as he carefully opened the flap.

Inside was a handwritten card. The paper was heavy, presumably expensive. On it, written in a delicate, almost calligraphic hand, was a short but clear message.

15

SHEREMETEV CASTLE, YURINO, RUSSIA

Father Lazarev gasped for breath when they finally pulled the stinking sack off his head. He looked around and realized that he was sitting handcuffed in a windowless room, surrounded by several armed men. The door opened. Another armed man entered and put a plate of food and a carafe of water on the table in front of him. He unlocked the handcuffs and motioned to the priest to eat.

As soon as he was done eating, Father Lazarev was again cuffed to the chair. Then his kidnapper came into the room and sat on a chair in front of him. Unlike the day before, however, when he had come across as cold and cruel, he now seemed amiable, even friendly.

"Hey, old man. If you like, I'll let you go today," he said.

"Where am I?" the priest asked.

"Oh, it's a lovely spot. Not so far from your home, in fact."

"Who are you? Why am I here?" Father Lazarev pressed.

"Listen closely, old man. We didn't bring you here to answer your questions, but for you to answer ours. Now, I'm not a barbarian. Allow me to introduce myself. My name is Heinrich von Falkenhain, and I have an assignment. You should know that I have a reputation for being conscientious and seeing any assignment I accept through to the end. I've never made an exception—and you, old man, will not be the first."

"What do you mean?"

"Here, today, you will reveal to me the secret you've been keeping all this time."

"I don't have any idea what you're talking about."

"You should know something else, old man. My reputation means a lot to me. As I said, I complete my assignments without fail. But just as important to me as my reputation is mutual respect. Do not take me for a fool."

Falkenhain stood up as he spoke, and just like that, his genial façade was gone. As if a switch had flipped, his voice turned hostile and his expression was suddenly savage. His face seemingly frozen, he glared at Father Lazarev. Not a muscle twitched. He did not blink. He stared at the priest and waited.

"I really don't—"

Without a breath of warning, the German's right fist shot forward and slammed into the old priest's face. The priest heard his nose shatter, felt blood pour down his face. A fraction of a second later, the left fist followed, then the right again. Father Lazarev's chair tipped over backward, but with his hands bound he could not even try to break his fall. The back of his head crashed against the stone floor, opening a wound, and a pool of blood immediately began to form. Two of the guards moved to set their prisoner upright again, but Falkenhain glowered at them, something insane in his eyes, making the two men stop in their tracks.

"Kitezh!" Falkenhain bellowed, like an animal gone wild, at the bleeding man lying on the floor. "Kitezh!"

Father Lazarev knew in that moment that it made no sense to go on pretending ignorance. The psychopath standing over him was capable of anything. Father Lazarev was torn, unsure what to do. He was the only person alive who knew the secret. If he let Falkenhain kill him, then it was lost forever.

"Kitezh! I want to know where it is, old man. No more games. None."

16

VIA DEGLI ACQUASPARTA, ROME

The message had been delivered. Now all he had to do was complete his preparations. He had studied his target's dossier to the last detail, and a man like Wagner would have no choice but to accept his invitation.

The assignment the man had accepted was certainly a challenge. Not only the actual shot, but the target himself. And now he had to factor in a certain amount of improvisation. The attack on Wagner had originally been planned for Vienna, but then Wagner had unexpectedly boarded a plane for Rome. Through contacts, however, the Kahle had managed to organize everything he needed at short notice.

He stopped on Via Degli Acquasparta and looked up at the theater in front of him, the Teatro Tordinona. The original building had been constructed four hundred years earlier, and had been rebuilt four times since; its current incarnation already had a good 140 years under its belt.

The Kahle slipped into the historical building through a side entrance and moved quickly and soundlessly up the stairs. The muffled strains of the last performance of the evening filled the narrow corridors. At the top floor, he silently broke the lock on the door that led higher still, to the rooftop level. To call it a tower would be an exaggeration, but the small room with leaded glass windows on all sides made a perfect sniper's nest.

The room was neglected and only used for storage. The layer of grime on the leaded windows made it almost impossible for him to see out. Some of the windowpanes even had newspaper pasted over them. *A pity, actually*, he thought. The view over the Tiber to the Palace of Justice on the opposite side was breathtaking. He set the backpack down on a table, took out the telescopic sight and crossed to the northeast window. The window was hinged in the middle and he tipped it up. He peered through the sight, tracing the length of Via Condotti, which led to one of the Rome's best-known tourist spots: the Spanish Steps. His target.

A complicated shot, the Kahle thought. One thousand two hundred meters through a canyon of buildings to a public square at the far end. But he had done his homework well and the weather was on his side. There was not a breath of wind. He had walked the length of the high-end retail street in the afternoon and had set out a few strategically placed little wind monitors that, on their own radio frequency, fed precise wind data to his ballistic calculator.

He pulled the table into the center of the room and assembled the rifle, then set it up on its bipod on the tabletop, the ballistic calculator and his mobile phone beside it. Using a glass cutter, he removed one of the panes from the leaded window to give himself a clear firing line at the height of the table. He pulled up an old wooden chair and sat down.

The display on his phone showed a blinking red dot on a map of Rome. His target was already on the way. The invitation was an extravagant gimmick, but it also had its pragmatic side: inside the heavy paper, he had concealed a small GPS transmitter. He could follow every step his target made.

He clicked the magazine into place and chambered a round. He read the ballistics data from the calculator and adjusted the telescopic sight accordingly. He was ready. He peered through the sight, keeping himself focused. Mr. Wagner was right on time. So predictable. The sniper reached for his phone and tapped the number on the screen.

17

TOM'S HOUSEBOAT, VIENNA

Hellen parked her car and climbed down the embankment to the shore of the Danube River. As she approached the houseboat moored at the river's edge, she admired the picture-perfect sunset. The sight brought back old memories. As reluctant as she was to admit it, the days when everything had still been good between her and Tom had been good days. Romantic evenings spent on the small veranda and walks alongside the Danube with the nighttime lights of the city glittering on the water. A new love in full bloom. It had been a carefree and lovely time. But as so often happened, reality and her job got in the way. And as wonderful as things had been between them at the start, the end had been ugly. But that made her all the happier that they had found a way to be around one another again, at least for now, in a more mature relationship, as friends.

She crossed the small gangplank, knocked on the door and tried to continue straight inside, but it suddenly and painfully became clear to her that the door was locked. She rubbed her bumped forehead in annoyance.

"*Un moment*," she heard from inside. A few seconds later, the door swung open and Cloutard welcomed her with a smile.

"Why is the door locked?" Hellen asked sharply, stepping briskly past Cloutard and into the houseboat.

"Why should the door not be locked?"

"Tom never locks his door!"

"But *chérie*, Tom is not here, and neither will I be for much longer. I must find another residence as soon as I can," Cloutard groaned. Hellen walked through the small living room, rummaging around a little. "Tom does not even have a decent bottle of cognac here, *un scandale totale*."

"Well, you *were* used to living in a fortress by the sea and having servants to satisfy your every wish. Your bathroom was probably bigger than Tom's houseboat."

Cloutard nodded, his face revealing his yearning for those long-lost days. "So true, *ma chère*, so true." Then softly, to himself, he added, "*Et je récupérai tout*—I will get it all back."

Hellen had stopped listening to Cloutard's murmuring. A silk scarf on a clothes rack had caught her eye, very clearly a woman's scarf. Hellen let the delicate fabric glide through her fingers.

"This is not exactly your color," she said to Cloutard. An odd feeling blossomed inside her. She was jealous. Did Tom have a girlfriend?

"It is also not mine," Cloutard replied, studiously ignoring the implied question in Hellen's words. He had no intention of getting caught bumbling between two opposing fronts. He put his hat on his head and with a sweep of his hand ushered Hellen back outside.

———

A short time later, Hellen's Mercedes CLA, her brand new company car, shot across the Reichsbrücke, the Imperial Bridge that led to the heart of Vienna. Passing north of the Prater park, she drove on toward Schwarzenbergplatz, where she could already see Schwarzenberg Palace rising beyond the Soviet War Memorial. Prinz-Eugen-Strasse led her along the park behind Schwarzenberg Palace, and a short distance further on was the famous Belvedere Palace. The palace had been built between 1714 and 1723 for Prince Eugen of Savoy, one of the Habsburg Empire's most prominent military commanders.

As a freelance journalist and war reporter, Tom's grandfather had made more than one lucrative deal for his pictures, and at the end of the 1980s he'd been approached by a publishing house. The result had a been a coffee-table book of his best work, which had sold countless copies worldwide since its release. This had brought him financial independence and an apartment with a view of Belvedere Palace, in the heart of Vienna's embassy district.

But not even ten years later, with the arrival of the internet and the rapid rise of digital photography, his profession had suffered a major setback. In certain circles, however, he was still counted among the greats.

"*Magnifique*. Vienna is truly one of the most beautiful cities in the world, *à l'exception de Paris*," Cloutard said with a sigh when Belvedere Palace came into view.

"It is. And this part of the city is pretty special. You could do far worse than having the palace park at my front door. Belvedere comes from the Italian for 'beautiful view,' you know."

Hellen turned the Mercedes into Theresianumgasse and began to look for somewhere to park. She was in luck; an open spot presented itself almost immediately.

"What do you think Tom's grandfather can tell us?" Cloutard asked as Hellen led the way to the old man's apartment building.

"I don't have the slightest idea. But if Tom says he saw the Cross of Kitezh in a photograph with his grandfather, let's hope it's a good story," Hellen said as they turned the corner into the Belvederegasse. She pointed to the building with the two lion sculptures flanking the iron gate.

"It's up there. It's been a long time since I saw the old man. I liked him a lot, but after Tom and I—"

She did not get to finish her sentence. An ear-splitting explosion followed instantly by a wave of heat swept Hellen and Cloutard off their feet. Shards of glass from dozens of windows shattered by the explosion rained down on them. Tongues of flame blazed from the building. Hellen's scream caught in her throat. Moments passed before what had just happened sank in.

"Oh my God . . ." she stammered. "That was his apartment."

18

CACIO E PEPE RESTAURANT, ROME

"Spanish Steps – 2300 – right stairway – foot of the street-lamp," the message said.

What was the cryptic invitation all about? Who sent it? Was it connected with Kitezh, or was it something else? Tom decided to be at the Spanish Steps at eleven, as stipulated, but he would keep his eyes open.

He checked his watch: just after ten. He took out his phone and opened the maps app. He'd been to Rome several times, but he was still a long way from being able to find his way around without assistance. The app told him he was a mile and a half from the steps. *A little stroll after a fantastic meal like that certainly won't hurt, either*, he thought as he left the restaurant.

When he reached the fountain at the base of the Spanish Steps, he checked the time again. In a few minutes, he hoped, he'd have answers to his questions. He made his way up the steps warily, looking around as he climbed, scanning the area. Despite the late hour, countless tourists were still out and about. At the first landing of the brightly lit stairway, he went to the streetlamp on the right, which stood on a stone plinth. He examined the elaborate cast-iron foot of the streetlamp and found a flip phone duct-taped underneath it, out of sight. As soon as he took the phone out, it rang. Taken aback by the timing, Tom flipped the phone open and lifted it to his ear. Was someone watching him?

"Welcome, Mr. Wagner." Tom's gut tightened—the man had mispronounced his name, but that at least revealed the first detail about the mysterious caller. The man spoke in accent-free High German. *So he's either from Hanover or he's just walked off stage at the National Theater*, Tom thought. The ludicrousness of the thought made him smile inwardly, but he stayed focused.

He looked around. Dozens of people were sitting around the edge of the fountain below, laughing and chatting. Everywhere he looked he saw tourists, and quite a few of them were on their phones. Which of them was "his" stranger? His eyes continued to roam.

"What's on your mind?" he said.

"Mr. Wagner, I've been asked by a mutual friend to pass on a message."

"You couldn't have just written it on the card? Why are we playing cat and mouse?" Tom said, his tone sharper. He kept looking around. Anyone with a phone in their hand was suspect. Something about the invitation in his pocket was bothering him, too, although he could not think why.

"Safety precautions. That, and I'm supposed to pass on the message in person," the man replied. He spoke slowly and deliberately.

"Okay. I'm here. Where are you?"

"Up on the next level."

From where he stood, Tom could see very little higher up. He slowly climbed the steps, his unease growing. He wound his way between tourists, his eyes switching from one to the next. Who was the caller?

"In the middle. Don't you see me?" the man asked. He sounded cynical.

Tom, in fact, did see a man with a phone to his ear. He headed toward him, but when he reached the center of the landing, the man suddenly hung up and hugged a girl who walked up to him just then. The two disappeared into the crowd.

Tom swung in a circle. The hairs on the back of his neck stood on end. He looked down at his feet for a moment, and he suddenly understood.

2300. No normal person would write the time like that. It was military. Tom's instincts shifted into full alarm mode.

"This is for Guerra," Tom heard, and his eyes widened.

19

SHEREMETEV CASTLE, YURINO, RUSSIA

"What are you talking about? No one knows where Kitezh is," the old priest groaned.

Within a heartbeat, Falkenhain metamorphosed again, making Father Lazarev shudder. The wild beast once again transformed into the outwardly calm negotiator. Two of the guards lifted the priest's chair upright again.

"No need to lie anymore, old man. I happen to know that you're the guardian. And I also know that you have not yet passed on your secret."

The priest smiled. "I don't have the least idea where you got this information, but I can assure you: you are mistaken. Or whoever told you I know the location was mistaken."

Falkenhain sighed, but remained calm, as if the outburst of a minute before had never happened. "But my task is to find out from you where Kitezh lies. And we have already established that I never leave an assignment uncompleted."

Falkenhain turned slowly to one of the guards and raised an eyebrow. The man immediately left the room only to return a moment later with an old leather bag, which he opened to reveal a range of metallic tools: knives, scalpels, nails, needles, hammers, shears and more.

Peter Lazarev knew where this was going. And it was true that he had not yet initiated his successor. Now he had to make a decision: die and take his knowledge to the grave, or reveal to his tormentor the secret that his family had preserved for centuries. But he could at least try to buy a little time. "What's the point? I know nothing. Torturing me won't change that."

"I'm not planning to torture just you, old man. I'm going to start with you, then move on to everyone you hold dear . . . I have time. Are you married? Then we'll bring your wife. Your son. Your daughter. Your grandson. And you'll see for yourself just how talented I am." Falkenhain ran his fingers lightly over the diverse instruments in front of him.

Father Lazarev inhaled sharply. He would not survive that, he knew. His own pain was one thing, but he would never be able to sit and watch this man torture his family.

Falkenhain grinned mockingly at him, until his cellphone rang and broke the malevolent silence. Falkenhain answered.

"Heinrich, have you got the priest?"

Falkenhain knew the voice on the line. He straightened up and squared his shoulders.

"Of course. He's sitting right in front of me," he answered quickly.

"Good. Has he said anything?"

"He denies all knowledge of the city. I think it's going to take a little time"—he looked into the priest's eyes—"but I have no doubt he'll tell me what we want to know quite soon."

"Do whatever you think is necessary. I know there's no one better than you, Heinrich, when it comes to talking stubborn people around. Just make sure he does not die."

"That goes without saying. I'm hardly going to touch a hair on his head." Again, Falkenhain stared at the bleeding priest.

"One more thing. There's someone else following the trail to Russia, a man named Tom Wagner. He's on his way to Nizhny Novgorod. He knows about Kitezh. We'll send you all the photos and information we have. I've crossed paths with him before. You can't afford to underestimate him."

"Naturally. I'll take care of it," Falkenhain said obsequiously.

"He'll be arriving soon. You can send a few of your people to watch him, then step in if he gets too close to us and our plans."

"Of course."

"I repeat: be careful. Do not underestimate this man."

Before Falkenhain could say another word, the caller had hung up.

Falkenhain put the phone away in his pocket and looked absently at the priest. He thought about Tom Wagner. He did not need to see any files about him. He knew who he was and what he was capable of. He had to be eliminated. Apart from himself, he knew only one other man he would trust to take Wagner out. So many others had already failed in the attempt. But that would not happen to him. He'd be the one to send Wagner to his grave, and he'd be the one to reap the reward. He and no one else.

He took out his phone again, tapped in a number and gave his orders. He knew how to deal with Wagner.

20

SPANISH STEPS, ROME

Screams. Panic. Blood. The crowds scattered in all directions. What happened? He had not heard a shot. He was lying on the ground. He looked at his hands, his shirt—he was covered in blood. But not his blood. In front of him lay a young man whose head had literally been blown apart. People cowered by the walls or lay flat on the ground. Some had taken cover behind the balustrade on the middle level of the steps. Some looked around for help. Other already had their phones out, filming.

Everything had happened in a split second. Tom had realized that he was standing atop a star-shaped relief set into the landing halfway up the Spanish Steps. With that and the military time on the invitation, he suddenly realized that a sniper had lured him into his crosshairs. He had dropped instantly and the bullet has missed him by a hair's breadth, taking the life of the unlucky young man who had been standing right next to him instead. He probably owed his life to the fact that lot could happen in the one second the bullet was in the air. *This is for Guerra*. He had run through many scenarios in his head, but that had not been among them. What did his parents' murderer, the man Tom himself had killed in Barcelona, have to do with Kitezh? Probably nothing. Okay, someone obviously knew he was in Rome, but who? Once the terror reports surrounding the Patriarch's visit to the Pope had turned out to be false, he had relaxed and let his guard down. He had wrongly connected the unknown attacker's message to the Kitezh story.

Tom stayed on the ground and crawled to the balustrade, where he could at least sit up. He still had the flip phone in his hand and raised it to his ear.

"You missed, asshole," he said. He looked back at the young man's body. From its position, he had an approximate idea of the direction from which the bullet must have come.

Next to Tom, a young woman cowered. She had also been showered by the victim's blood, and she now sat staring into empty space in shock and fear, her entire body trembling. In her hand she held one of the new mega-zoom cameras, the kind of thing you could use to photograph a fly on a wall from a hundred yards away.

"Mind if I borrow that?" Tom whispered.

The girl barely reacted when Tom lifted the camera out of her hand.

"You have one option, Mr. Wagner," the sniper said, his voice horribly calm.

"And that would be?" Tom was trying to keep the killer wherever he was. He had to give himself a chance to figure out the sniper's position. He raised the camera above the balustrade and used the monitor to scour the area in the direction from which the shot had come, searching frantically, and quickly spotted the small tower at the end of Via Condotti. Even from there, he could make out the hole in the window. He could not see the rifle, but he knew that a good sharpshooter always shot from inside. It had to be the sniper's nest. Unfortunately, it was too far away. By the time he got close, the killer would have long since vanished.

"Here's what's going to happen. I'm going to shoot tourists at random until you accept your inevitable fate." He paused to let that sink in, then said, "I'll show you what I mean. See the woman in yellow?"

Tom didn't even have time to draw breath to shout a warning. He did not hear the shot, but the woman's head exploded and her body collapsed. The projectile slammed into the stone wall, sending chips of concrete flying in all directions. A chorus of screams rose from the crowd and the panicked whimpers grew louder.

"You cold-blooded fuck. When I get my hands on you, you'll suffer," Tom snarled into the phone.

The killer laughed at Tom's courage. "You have three seconds."

"Stop. Just wait. Please!" Tom's voice started to crack.

He saw only one way out. He took a deep breath and drew his Glock.

"Okay, I'm coming out." From cover, he shot out the two streetlamps closest to him. Then he jumped to his feet and quickly and methodically shot out one lamp after the other. The steps fell into darkness almost instantly.

"*Andiamo!*" Tom yelled, the only word that came to him. He shouted it at the top of his lungs, trying to get the people around him to move, to run away, which they finally began to do. They ran up, down, anywhere to get to safety. Tom, too, ran higher up the steps, and lifted the phone to his ear one last time.

"I'm going to find you and make you pay."

"I'm impressed, Mr. Wagner. You win round one, but we'll talk again." The line went dead.

Tom used the chaos to disappear. At the top of the steps he reached the Piazza di Spagna and ran to the right. A Vespa lay in the middle of the street, its motor still running. The owner was cowering behind a parked car. Tom lifted the Vespa onto its wheels, swung onto the saddle and twisted the throttle. The owner didn't even have time to protest.

At full speed, Tom raced along Via Sistina against the one-way traffic. All around him, people were running. When he reached the next intersection the street switched directions, and he was at least moving in the same direction as the rest of the traffic. Then he saw a sign: 'Roma Termini.' He hadn't been to Rome's main train station for than a year. It wasn't the most attractive part of the city. As in most big cities, the area around the station was crawling with the homeless, with drug dealers and prostitutes. The perfect place to go into hiding. He ditched the Vespa in a side street, washed his face at a small fountain and disappeared down a dark alleyway. He had to keep moving. When he felt he could stop and catch his breath, he took out his phone. There was only one person in Rome he felt he could turn to.

21

SOMEWHERE IN ROME

He'd been out of the bustling tourist parts of Rome for more than an hour, but it felt like an eternity. His phone had long since given up the ghost, and in his desperation he'd literally bought the hooded sweatshirt off a junkie's back. He couldn't wander through the city looking like a walking Jackson Pollock painting, so he had handed over his last fifty euros for the stinking, ragged sweatshirt. He'd had no other choice. Now he was on foot, picking a path through backstreets to reach their rendezvous.

For a brief moment, he'd been tempted to call Lorenzo Da Silva and tell him the whole story, but he couldn't stand the guy and that was reason enough not to trust him. He didn't want to get the Pope involved, which left only one person in Rome he could rely on—Sister Lucrezia. He'd met the Mother Superior and the three younger nuns in her charge more than a year earlier. Their paths had crossed more than once since then, and they had been through quite a lot together.

Tom was standing in the shadows at the rendezvous when the old, bright-red Alfa Romeo Autotutto van he knew so well rolled to a stop beside him. Behind the wheel of the beautifully maintained vintage van sat Sister Lucrezia.

On the back seat behind her sat Sister Bartolomea. She opened the side door and cried, "Tom! Get in!"

Surprised that Sister Lucrezia had already managed to gather reinforcements, he quickly climbed inside. Sister Lucrezia hit the gas.

"I don't know how many favors I owe you," Tom said.

"None at all," said Sister Lucrezia. "We will always be in your debt." Tom leaned back on the seat and heaved a sigh of relief. He was finally off the street, at least, and for some reason he felt perfectly safe whenever he was around the nuns.

"What hornet's nest have you been stirring up now, Signor Tom?" Sister Bartolomea asked.

"I wish I knew. I don't have a clue what's going on. First we find the Cross of Kitezh on St. Peter's Tomb and the next moment a stone-cold killer is shooting at me and innocent bystanders in the name of Guerra."

"For all that, you don't look too bad." Sister Bartolomea waved her hand in front of her nose. "But you should really get changed. Get rid of that pullover as soon as you can. With fire, preferably," she said, plucking at Tom's newly purchased sweatshirt.

"Guerra . . . he was that horrible man in Barcelona, wasn't he?" said Sister Lucrezia.

"Yeah. And apparently someone's got a score to settle with me on his account, presumably the organization whose plans I screwed up back then. I don't think they're my biggest fans." He smiled tiredly.

"By the way, you're a YouTube star," Sister Bartolomea said, holding out her phone for him to see.

Tom's face froze. Unbelievable: someone at the Spanish Steps had filmed him. The grainy video showed a blood-covered man—him—firing a pistol in all directions and screaming "Andiamo!" The video was colorfully titled "Crazy gun-toting tourist runs amok in Rome!"

"When you told me what had happened, I checked online," said Sister Lucrezia. "Things happen so fast these days, you know. And that's what I found."

"But no one's going to recognize you in the video, thank the Lord. Not with all that blood on your face," Sister Bartolomea said, doing her best to console Tom. He feigned a smile, the best he could manage.

"We brought your things," Sister Lucrezia said, and Sister Bartolomea pointed to Tom's gray duffel in the back of the van. "The Holy Father was able to contact the Patriarch in time. He said he could take you with him to Nizhny Novgorod. His plane is flying under diplomatic protection and they're waiting for you at the airport."

"We're taking you straight there," Sister Bartolomea added.

"You shouldn't have brought the Pope into this," Tom protested.

"He was more than happy to help. He always will be, you know that."

Tom nodded.

"We'll be there in a few minutes. You really should put on something fresh." Sister Bartolomea pulled the duffel forward for Tom, but he only sat and gazed out into the night, lost in thought. He sensed that this was only the beginning. He could not explain what the attempt on his life had to do with Kitezh. Suddenly, like an electric shock, it hit him: Hellen, Cloutard and his grandfather were very likely in danger, too.

22

ARTHUR JULIUS PREY'S APARTMENT, VIENNA

The devastation was immense. Countless windows in the surrounding buildings had shattered and flames leapt from Tom's grandfather's apartment. Car alarms screamed. Fire engines, police and emergency vehicles rapidly blocked the narrow street. The building's residents had been quickly evacuated and now stood behind the police barrier. Several of them needed treatment for smoke and injuries. Rubberneckers joined neighbors at the police tape, and curious faces watched from buildings all around.

The fire truck ladders were being retracted as the firefighters, air tanks on their backs, left the building. The fire was out, but steam and smoke still drifted skyward.

"Tell me again exactly what happened and how you know Mr. Prey," the officer talking to Hellen said, and she told him in a few words what she and Cloutard had witnessed.

" . . . and Mr. Prey is the grandfather of a friend of mine. Tom Wagner. He's ex-Cobra. Maybe you know him."

"Oh, yeah. Waaaagner," the officer said with disdain. "Yeah, we all know him."

Hellen narrowed her eyes and continued. "Anyway, Tom's in Rome just now, on assignment at the Vatican. He asked me to look in on his grandfather while he was away. He's an old man, after all."

She had made up her mind to keep their true reason for visiting Tom's grandfather to herself, but thinking about the nice old man made Hellen sad. For her, he would always be Grandpop Arti. How was she supposed to tell Tom that his last family member in the world was dead? Cloutard saw the pain on her face. He put one arm around her shoulders and gave her a reassuring hug.

The fire chief joined them and signaled to the policeman that he wanted to talk. "Excuse me for a moment," the officer said, and he turned away to talk to the chief.

"The fire's out," Hellen heard the chief say. "But it looks like someone triggered a bomb up there. And if you ask me, whoever it was ransacked the place before that. We're referring the case to the arson unit. Seal off everything. No one's to go near the apartment."

Hellen and Cloutard looked at each other in shock. "Who in God's name would want to kill Grandpop Arti?" Hellen said softly to Cloutard. "The Cross of Kitezh suddenly appears and someone tries to kill Tom's grandfather? That can't be a coincidence, especially if Tom thinks his grandfather might know something about the cross." She raised her voice again: "If that's all, we'll be going. We have to let a good friend know that his grandfather's been murdered," Hellen said, a lump forming in her throat. "You have my number," she added, and turned away.

The fire chief was just leaving, and the policeman turned his attention back to Hellen and Cloutard. "Murdered? Why murdered? They didn't find any human remains in the apartment, just what was left of a cat. We'll be in touch if we have any more questions."

Another surprise. "If Tom's *Grand-père* was not at home, then where is he?" Cloutard asked.

"Good question," Hellen said, just as puzzled as Cloutard.

They walked slowly back toward the car. Hellen said a little prayer of thanks that she had parked around the corner, or they would have had a much harder time escaping this chaos quickly.

"Maybe we should ask the neighbors if anyone knows where—" Hellen began, but as they ducked beneath the police tape, an elderly woman reached out and touched her arm.

"Excuse me, young lady, are you by any chance looking for Mr. Prey?"

"Yes!" Hellen said, and her expression brightened instantly.

"Oh, how lovely. I thought you might be, because you looked very familiar to me. You're the grandson's girlfriend, aren't you? I haven't see you here for a very long time. You really ought to come and visit Arthur, I mean,

Mr. Prey, more often," the old lady said, a finger lifted in reprimand.

Hellen blushed a little. She had neither the time nor the desire to talk about her love life with a stranger.

"Do you know where Mr. Prey is?"

"Of course. He's on vacation in Cuba," the old woman said. Then she lowered her voice to a whisper and winked at Hellen as she added, "He's visiting his sweetheart! I'm looking after his cat while he's away."

"*Je suis désolé*. The cat, I am afraid to say, did not survive the explosion," Cloutard said, putting on a very French accent.

Hellen rolled her eyes. "Do you know how we can reach him? Mr. Prey, I mean."

The old woman smiled and, to Hellen's astonishment, she took an iPhone out of handbag and navigated with surprising skill to an email that Tom's grandfather had sent her.

"My granddaughter gave me this phone, you know. It took me a little while, but I think I'm slowly starting to get the hang of it. We do a lot of that Face-thingy together, you know. Here, look." She smiled broadly and held out the phone to Hellen.

Hellen quickly read the email.

"May I forward this?" she asked. The old woman nodded and Hellen quickly sent the email on to herself and Cloutard. She thanked the old woman and handed back her phone. Then she hooked her arm under Cloutard's and pulled him along with her.

"Tell young Tom he should visit his grandfather more often," the old woman called behind them, waving.

When they had moved away a little, Hellen said, "If this really was a bomb, then Tom's grandfather is still in grave danger."

"Leave it to me," Cloutard said. "I have good contacts in Cuba. South America used to be an excellent, shall we say, hunting ground. And Cuba was always a good place to hide. You fly to Russia and I will make sure nothing happens to the old *charmeur*."

As they turned the corner out of sight, a man stepped from an apartment block entrance and headed straight for the old woman who had just been talking to them.

23

PEARL CONTINENTAL HOTEL, KARACHI, PAKISTAN

The delicate hand worked its way along the Welshman's neck, kneading his shoulder muscles so forcefully that he had to grit his teeth and concentrate to stop himself from screaming in pain. It never failed to amaze him that such fine hands, attached to such a petite, fragile-seeming body, could contain so much strength. He had found the diminutive Thai woman ten years earlier in the slums of Bangkok, in the port area of Khlong Toei. She had been twelve years old at the time, living alone in filth and poverty and on the edge of starvation. He had made up his mind to rescue her from the slums—he had always had a soft spot for Thai women, although even after ten years her name simply would not stick in his head. Over the years, she had become his servant, his lover, his masseuse, and sometimes his assistant and adviser as well.

She had almost finished with the daily, two-hour massage when the Welshman's cell phone rang. The woman dutifully interrupted the massage, reached for the phone and glanced at the display.

"This is important," she said, somewhere between an observation and a command. The young woman and the Welshman, over the years, had developed a unique relationship. The Welshman sighed, sat up on the massage table and answered the call. While he talked, the woman went to work lower down.

"I hope for your sake the old man talked," the Welshman said.

There was silence on the other end of the line. The Welshman knew what that meant. It was a few seconds before the caller could bring himself to reply.

"No, sir. We can't a word out of him. We're going to have to use other methods. Friedrich is an expert in special interrogation techniques, as you know."

The Welshman let out a low groan as the massage began to take effect and blood flowed from his brain to a part of his body where it was more urgently needed. The caller dutifully ignored the groan.

"No. The man is old. He would not survive the German's special treatment for long. We have other options for getting the answers we need, fortunately. Plan B is on track?"

"Yes, sir. Everything is going just as you planned." The caller paused as if he had to summon all his courage to formulate what he had to say next. "Sir, we believe it is necessary for you to be here in person. Our communication options here are very limited. When things really start to move, we will have to decide quickly. It would be good to have you here for that. You are also the only one able to keep Friedrich in check. The man is good, but he's a bomb with a short fuse."

The Welshman nodded. His masseuse was making considerable progress with her own "special techniques" and it was becoming an effort just to string a complete sentence together. He had to wind up this call as fast as he could.

"All right. I'll be on the next plane," he said and hung up. He looked down at the girl and had just closed his eyes to give himself over completely to the final pleasure when the door flew open and Qadir, his right-hand man, burst into the room.

The young woman shrieked and jumped away, and the Welshman hastily covered himself with a towel, although it did little to hide the consequence of the intimate massage. But it was not the first time Qadir had witnessed such a scene, and he ignored it completely.

"Sahib, we have a big problem. We'll have to hurry if we want to get the treasure out of Kitezh safely."

The Welshman was suddenly all ears. As his servant and fix-it man, Qadir was the only one allowed to interrupt anytime and anywhere, his only confidante able to judge the true urgency of a situation. The Welshman trusted him unreservedly. Qadir handed him a sheet of paper.

"The seismographic readings from the area around Nizhny Novgorod. Something big is coming."

It took the Welshman a few seconds to interpret the data. Then he jumped from the massage table as if stung by a scorpion. The towel fell to the floor, but he didn't care. He turned to Thai woman. "Pack our things. We have to get to Russia, fast!"

24

THERESIA DE MEY'S APARTMENT, CENTRAL VIENNA

"We need the jet," Hellen said. On second thought, it probably wasn't the best opening, considering she had just woken the head of Blue Shield up in the middle of the night—even if the head of Blue Shield was her own mother.

Hellen and Cloutard had driven straight from Arthur Prey's bombed-out apartment to see Theresia de Mey at home, but once Hellen had briefed her mother about the Cross of Kitezh and the attack on Tom's grandfather, Theresia agreed to approve an official Blue Shield investigation. But on one condition: at the end of the day, Hellen had to have something concrete to show for it.

"The budget we get from UNESCO is not enough for what I want my Blue Shield to be," Theresia de Mey said. "Yes, we had a little windfall after your last escapade. But the UNO, in its infinite wisdom, has now decided it can put that money to better use elsewhere. So we are in a tight spot, financially speaking. Bring me something with actual monetary or historical value, something I can present to the world. Blue Shield has to find private investors to survive. Thanks to Monsieur Cloutard I have enough contacts, at least for now. All legal, too, astonishingly enough. But I need to be able to show them something extraordinary. I hate to say it, but this is the price we have to pay to protect the cultural treasures of this world.

"And by the way, when you see Mr. Wagner, tell him that was the last time I will put up with him running off the way he did. And ask him to have a word with his friend in Rome. I've had a number of inquiries. Interested parties from New York to Tokyo would pay well to be able to put the Sword of Peter on display, but the Vatican seems to have no interest whatsoever."

Hellen nodded obediently and turned to go.

"And darling? Next time, just call." With that, Theresia de Mey closed the door behind her daughter.

———

"I will arrange my visa myself, *Chérie*," Cloutard said when Vittoria ran through the details of his flight. Vittoria Arcano, former Interpol agent and now Theresia de Mey's right hand, had already worked out everything else—and getting a flight plan together for a private jet on such short notice was no easy task.

En route to the airport, they had made brief stops at Tom's houseboat and Hellen's apartment to pick up a few items. Hellen still had a few hours before her flight left, but she saw no sense in driving back into the city after she had dropped Cloutard at the private terminal.

A short time later, Cloutard was Havana-bound and making himself at home in the Blue Shield jet. He put his feet up, poured himself a small glass of his favorite cognac and leaned back in the oversized leather seat. *Ah, the good old days*, he thought, sipping his cognac with delight. Theresia de Mey had been nice enough to equip the minibar of the Blue Shield jet with Louis XIII. The luxurious Gulfstream V had come into Blue Shield's possession indirectly, seized by Interpol as part of a drug raid—Theresia de Mey had gotten herself a jet at a bargain-basement price.

25
STRIGINO AIRPORT, NIZHNY NOVGOROD

"Can you explain this?"

Hellen held out her phone, showing Tom the video of him in his blood-splattered T-shirt, firing wildly in all directions. It was mid-morning and Tom had arrived in time to meet Hellen at arrivals. Now they were waiting for her suitcase to appear.

"Amazing how good the cameras are on these new phones, amiright?" Tom said. He tapped on one part of the screen. "See? Only one streetlamp lit and you can still see it's me. Okay, it's grainy and I'm covered in blood, but I'm still impressed."

Hellen raised one eyebrow. She looked at Tom but said nothing. He knew that look: she was through joking around. "Okay, the short version," he sighed, and explained to Hellen what had happened.

"How do you keep getting dragged into these insanely absurd situations? You're a catastrophe magnet! More happens to you in a week than happens to normal people in their entire lives."

"Is it my fault if people keep shooting at me? The guy was a stone-cold contract killer, very professional. But more importantly, did you visit Grandpop?"

Hellen's face was suddenly stricken. Tom knew that look, too, and he suspected the worst.

"Is he okay?"

Hellen explained what had happened in Vienna and immediately tried to put Tom's mind at ease: "François is on his way to Havana. He'll look after Arti."

"Is François really the right guy for the job?" Tom did not feel very reassured. He and Cloutard had been through more than one escapade together, but he also knew the Frenchman's criminal past and that he could switch allegiances at the drop of his Panama hat. He could only hope that Cloutard would find his grandfather and keep an eye on him.

"Tom, don't forget that your grandfather can also take care of himself pretty well. I remember the stories he told us about his time as a war reporter."

He had to admit that she was right. There was little he could do anyway, at least for now.

"Okay, Professor de Mey. Tell me more about this 'invisible city'."

Hellen smiled. She didn't need to be asked twice. Her eyes bright with enthusiasm, she launched into the history of Kitezh, and Tom could see that she was in her element. "Of course. Well, at the start of the 13th century, there were two cities: Maly Kitezh, which means Little Kitezh, and Bolshoi Kitezh, or Big Kitezh."

"Bolshoi? I hope you're not taking me to the ballet. God, anything but that. Do you remember the time you dragged me to the State Opera?"

"Yes! You snored so loud the usher came and threw us out. It took me months to get decent tickets again. Don't worry, no ballet."

Tom breathed with relief.

"So, according to legend, Little Kitezh was founded by the Grand Prince of Vladimir," Hellen said.

"By the lake where they say it sank?"

"Actually, no. Little Kitezh was on the shores of the Volga River, not far from Nizhny Novgorod. But then the same Grand Prince of Vladimir discovered a much more beautiful location on the shores of Lake Svetloyar, and that's where he built Big Kitezh. The city quickly became known as a holy site, like the Vatican, and there were churches, monasteries and palaces built all around the city."

"So what happened to it?" Tom asked.

"Genghis Khan's grandson, that's what," said Hellen.

"What do you mean?"

"In 1238, Batu Khan, Genghis Khan's grandson, led the Mongol armies into the northeastern part of Russia. While his soldiers were conquering, plundering and burning everything in their path, including Little Kitezh, the Khan heard about Big Kitezh, and suddenly he had a new goal. All that mattered to him from that moment on was taking the city."

"But didn't Genghis Khan have hundreds of grandchildren?" Tom asked.

"Yes, but only one of them ever amounted to anything. That was Batu. The Grand Prince tried to negotiate with Batu Khan, but he ended up having to flee for his life when the Khan tried to have him killed. The problem was that none of the Khan's soldiers knew the exact location of Big Kitezh. So he interrogated his prisoners from Little Kitezh."

"Did they tell him?"

"No. Not one of them would reveal the holy city's location, which made the Khan furious. He ordered the prisoners to be beaten and tortured but still none of them said a word."

"Why not? Weren't they scared? Why were they so loyal?" Tom was curious now, and Hellen grinned. She could tell that he was getting interested.

"They were more afraid of the eternal curse of Kitezh than they were of death threats and torture."

"The eternal curse . . .?"

"Yes. The prisoners believed that if they revealed the location of Big Kitezh they would bring down a curse on themselves and their descendants forever."

"So if none of them told the Khan where the city was, how did the Mongols find it?"

"In the end, one of the prisoners finally broke. They tortured him beyond human endurance, and he told them about the secret routes that led to Lake Svetloyar."

"What happened to the Grand Prince?"

"They say he died in the battle. Before he died, though, he was able to hide all of the city's holy artifacts and treasures in the lake. Then, somehow, the city became . . . invisible. No one really knows today exactly how to interpret that, or what 'the invisible city' really means. These days, all there is at Lake Svetloyar is the lake itself and lots of forest."

"So no one really knows what became of Kitezh?" Tom raised his eyebrows. He hoped they had not flown all this way for nothing.

"They say that the city is only visible to the pure of heart, and that those who truly believe in it can hear church bells coming from the lake. Some even claim to have seen the outlines of buildings on the lakebed."

"But no one's really seen or heard anything?"

"No. Several archeological expeditions have studied the area around the lake, and they have found signs of an old settlement. But no relics or treasures. The Kitezh mythology also says that all of Batu Khan's plunder is also to be found in the city—and it was a long campaign that cut right across the heart of Asia."

"Do you think there's a chance we'll find anything new?"

"Honestly, I have no idea. But it's too tempting not to at least try."

While Hellen was relating the history of Kitezh, her luggage arrived. Three minutes later, they were sitting in Tom's rental car on their way into the city.

"By the way, we have to get you an outfit for tonight," Tom said casually.

Hellen frowned. "An outfit?"

"Unless you have an evening dress packed in your suitcase."

"Why would I need an evening dress?"

"The Patriarch has invited us to Nizhny Novgorod's kremlin. They're celebrating the city's eighth centenary. Even the Russian president's going to be there."

"The Pope, the American president, the Russian president. The speed-dial list on your phone must be bursting at the seams," Hellen said with a smile, and Tom once again sensed the attraction that still existed between them.

"True. But I think I could still find a slot for the Dalai Lama," he said.

———

Twelve hours after leaving Vienna, the pilot opened the door of the Gulfstream and lowered the steps. Tiny beads of sweat appeared instantly on Cloutard's forehead as he stepped out of the air-conditioned interior of the plane.

Sun, sea, a cloudless sky, cocktails, music and a unique lust for life – that was Cuba. Cloutard straightened his Panama hat as he descended the steps, then looked up to see a bright red Chevy convertible parked on the airport apron. The vintage beast was still in good shape, but it wore its seventy years of history on its sleeve. A copper-tanned man leaned against the driver's door, puffing on a fat cigar—an unusual sight: most locals could hardly afford cigars. But Cirilo García López was no regular Cuban. He served as a kind of ambassador, a link in the chain between corrupt government officialdom and organized crime.

Cirilo threw up his arms when he saw Cloutard and came to meet him, the cigar pushed into the corner of his mouth.

"*Hola* François. Welcome back," Cirilo shouted happily.

"*Salut*, old friend. So good to see you again."

The two men threw their arms around each other in a brotherly embrace, then Cirilo took Cloutard's bag and put it on the white-leather back seat of the convertible.

"I see you still have your old *fotingo*." The Cubans used the word, which translated roughly as "jalopy," with affection to describe the vintage cars that were an inseparable part of the cityscape of Havana.

"*Si, compañero*. She has never let me down," Cirilo said and he rapped his knuckles on the door. They climbed in and the car trundled toward the airport exit. The boom gate swung upwards and the guard waved them through.

"Getting into Cuba with your help is still as smooth as silk, I see," Cloutard said, patting his old friend on the shoulder.

"*Pero seguro*. Except it is a little more expensive than it used to be." Cirilo rubbed his fingers together and they both laughed. "By the way, I have a gift for you." Cirilo reached over to the back seat and came back with a beautifully made cylindrical wooden box in his hand. He passed it to Cloutard.

Cloutard's eyes widened.

"Is this ...?"

"*Siiii!*" Cirilo smiled.

Cloutard opened the box reverently. "Havana Club Maximo Extra Añejo," Cloutard whispered, examining the expensive Baccara decanter. The strictly limited special edition cost almost two thousand dollars a bottle—a lot of money for half a liter of rum.

"You do know that I have lost my empire and that I am not able to afford such luxuries right now?"

"Don't worry, *viejo amigo*," Cirilo said reassuringly. "*Lo siento mucho*. We could not believe it when we heard the news."

"Thank you. But do not worry. I will get it all back."

―――

Half an hour later, Cirilo and Cloutard were driving along the Malecón, Havana's famous esplanade. The Malecón led them past *La Habana Vieja*—Old Havana, the city's tourist hotspot and a gorgeous piece of the island's history. Since 1982 it had also been a UNESCO World Heritage Site. The old buildings were gradually being renovated, but there were still more than enough of the ramshackle buildings that characterized the city.

They continued along the Malecón past Castillo de San Salvador de la Punta until they reached Castillo de la Real Fuerza. Just past the fortress complex, they turned into a small cul-de-sac and Cirilo stopped the car at the end.

"Your friend lives up there, top floor." Cirilo pointed. Cloutard looked up at the green-and-yellow building, overlooking Plaza de Armas on one side and the harbor on the other. It stood opposite a small garden and adjacent to a public library, and was definitely among Old Havana's more attractive buildings. The white wooden shutters, closed to the heat of the day, and the encircling balcony on the top floor only added to the charm of the house.

Cloutard got out of the car and went to the entrance of the building, which faced a small municipal garden adjacent to a public library. Inside, he climbed the narrow staircase, which was sorely in need of renovation. At the end of the hallway was the apartment. He looked around and was about to knock when he heard sounds from inside. He put his ear to the door and heard thumping and a clattering sound, then muffled whimpering and murmurs.

He knocked on the door.

26

ARMANI STORE, NIZHNY NOVGOROD

Tom had never had much time for style or designer clothing, but as he inspected himself in the mirror, he had to admit he looked pretty good. Hellen had disappeared into the ladies' section, giving Tom the opportunity to clear his head.

Hellen was the only woman Tom had ever truly loved. Unfortunately for both of them, the balance between their differences and their passion for one another had tipped; in time the drama had become too much. Deep down, they were two very different people, and there were just too many ways they didn't fit together. After they broke up, Tom had sworn that he would never again let anyone get as close to him as Hellen had. Everything about love confused the hell out of him.

And yet here he was, with Hellen in Russia, buying expensive designer clothes for an evening they were going to spend together. Not a date, of course. No, this was purely professional. At least, Tom tried to tell himself it was.

He heard a soft whistle as he appraised himself in the mirror. "James Bond would die of envy, I'm sure," Hellen said. "Although he always preferred Brioni. You'll have to get rid of the five-o'clock shadow, and that mop on your head isn't exactly what I'd expect on a gentleman...but other than that, a woman could almost be seen in public with you." The words were friendly, but the tone was a little cool. It bothered him, but he couldn't quite put his finger on why.

He turned around and his jaw dropped. Hellen was wearing a stunning black dress, the picture of elegance and femininity. Flounces adorned the back of the close-fitting, sleeveless garment, while the neckline dipped low, accentuating and hinting at what was underneath—a simple dress, but incredibly sexy.

He had to admit that she looked breathtaking, and he told her so. But she still seemed distant. Too much had happened in the last year. *It's probably better this way*, he told himself. *We don't want to start all that madness again.*

Hellen paid with her Blue Shield credit card and the assistant packed their new outfits into stylish shopping bags.

"Do you think tonight could be dangerous?" Hellen asked. "Just so I can prepare." She did not sound concerned at all.

"I doubt it. No one knows the cross has turned up."

Hellen was all business, and as they left the store it bothered Tom that she hadn't been receptive to even his slightest compliment. He decided to give it up. It made no sense, anyway. Outside, Tom flagged down a taxi to take them back to the hotel.

"That guy was kind of strange, wasn't he?" Tom said after Hellen had passed the hotel's business card to the driver.

"I can hardly wait to actually see the cross for real," Hellen said distractedly, looking for maybe the fiftieth time at the picture of the cross on her phone. It took her several seconds to realize that Tom had asked her a question. "Which guy?"

"You were miles away, weren't you?" Hellen looked at him, not understanding. "The whole time we were in the shop, there was only one other customer."

"So?"

"Well, he was completely bald. And I mean completely. A real cue ball. No hair, no eyebrows, not even eyelashes."

"The things you notice when a woman in a sexy evening dress is standing right in front of you," Hellen said, and she sighed. "Times change, I guess."

27

ARTHUR JULIUS PREY'S APARTMENT, HAVANA, CUBA

"Monsieur Prey? Hallo?"

No answer.

Cloutard knocked again, then reached for the door handle. To his surprise, the door was not locked. *Is it something in Tom's genes?* he briefly wondered. Cautiously, he stepped inside. Behind the door, a baseball bat leaned against the wall, and he smiled as he picked it up. Armed now, he crept deeper into the small, shabby apartment. The noises were coming from a room at the back. Cloutard was not sure if the place was just messy or if someone had ransacked it. He advanced with caution. In the past, he had rarely had a direct hand in anything—he had had people for that sort of thing. But that had all been in another life. He positioned himself in front of the door from behind which the sounds were coming, took a firm grip on the bat, and kicked the door open.

"Oh, *mon Dieu!*" Cloutard exclaimed. It took him a split second to process the scene in front of him, then he instantly turned away and closed the door behind him. But he was too late: the image had burned itself onto his brain. Arthur Prey, Tom's grandfather—surprisingly sprightly for his seventy-five years, as Cloutard had just discovered—was in the middle of a stormy lovemaking session involving his Cuban girlfriend and a chest of drawers, his pants around his ankles. The wobbly piece of furniture, the old man's puffing, and the pleasure-filled squeals of the woman, some years younger than Arthur, had let Cloutard to fatally misinterpret the situation. Chattering in Spanish and frantic thumping came from the other side of the door, and Tom's grandfather appeared seconds later brandishing a revolver.

"Who the devil are you?" he shouted, the gun leveled at Cloutard's head. Cloutard immediately dropped the baseball bat and raised his hands in the air.

"I am a friend of your grandson, Tom Wagner. My name is François Cloutard. I work for Blue Shield with Tom and Hellen de Mey."

"Hellen? I thought they'd broken up?"

In as few words as possible, Cloutard explained to the old man what had happened.

"Artjom," Arthur whispered. "I haven't heard from him in years." He slumped onto a chair at the kitchen table and put the revolver aside. "And my cat?"

Cloutard squeezed his eyes closed and shook his head.

The bedroom door opened a little and the Cuban woman peeped out through the gap. She had wrapped herself in a sheet.

"*No hay nada de malo?*" she whispered. Then she came out of the room and dashed to Arthur. She laid her hand on his shoulder and kissed him on the cheek.

"This is Aniel," Arthur said by way of introduction.

"*Enchantée*," said Cloutard.

"*Mi nieto necesita me ayuda*—my grandson needs my help," Arthur said to Aniel. "Get dressed, we have to leave." He turned to Cloutard. "I have to get something first."

"What do you have to get?" Cloutard asked in surprise. "We have to get to Russia as fast as we can. Someone has already destroyed your apartment in Vienna and you are in great danger here."

"Maybe so, but if this is really about Father Lazarev and the cross he showed me forty years ago, then there is something we have to go and get. Trust me."

Tom's grandfather did not give the impression of being seventy-five years old. He was as fit as a man half his age and wore a full gray beard that reminded Cloutard of Ernest Hemingway.

Cloutard's phone rang. "Cirilo," he read on the display, and he took the call.

"I don't know what you're involved in, but two evil-looking bastards just jumped out of a car down here and they're heading for your uncle's building. Something tells me they're here for him. Get the hell out of there as fast as you can."

28
KREMLIN OF NIZHNY NOVGOROD

"I had no idea there was a kremlin outside Moscow," Tom said as he climbed out of the taxi and looked up at the fortress, originally built in the sixteenth and seventeenth centuries. Thousands of people were streaming toward the citadel to be part of the celebration of the city's eight-hundredth birthday.

"There are many kremlins in Russia, in fact, but the one in Moscow is the best known. The kremlins are citadels that were built on the borders of the Grand Duchy of Moscow to protect it from raiders. Part of the construction of this particular kremlin is ascribed to the Italian architect Pietro Frjasin. Its walls are a mile and a half in length and up to forty feet high, with thirteen watch-towers built in."

Tom took the tickets that the Patriarch had given him out of his jacket pocket and showed them to the security guards at the main entrance. They passed through an airport-like security check followed by a thorough patting down, but Hellen wasn't about to let anything dampen her enthusiasm. She went on telling Tom about the complex.

"There are also five large square towers that used to be topped by artillery pieces. Each tower has its own name, similar to other kremlins. That one there, for example," —she pointed to a tower some distance to their right— "is the Demetrievskaya Tower. Its name comes from a church sanctified to Demetrius of Thessaloniki that used to stand opposite the tower."

From security they made their way through a parking area toward the concert hall.

"That doesn't look particularly historical," Tom said, pointing to an ugly prefabricated concrete building.

"It's not. In the Soviet era in the 20th century, several administration buildings were constructed on the kremlin grounds. In World War Two, the roofs of the Taynitskaya, Severnaya and Chasovaya towers were dismantled and replaced with anti-aircraft guns on platforms. And that there"—Hellen pointed to a white-painted church with a green roof—"is the Archangel Cathedral, which dates back to the sixteenth century. There was an older building here before this one, dating from 1227. It was one of the first religious structures in Russia made of stone."

Tom was impressed. A year earlier he would not have found any of it especially interesting. Art, culture and history had never matter much to him. But the adventures of the last year had awakened a fascination in him for historical myths, antique artifacts and sunken treasure.

"The things you know," he murmured admiringly as they stepped into the foyer of the concert hall. At the entrance to the kremlin, Tom had noted the presence of hundreds of police and military vehicles. An eighth centennial celebration was a big deal, no doubt, but did it call for marching an entire company around inside the kremlin walls?

Tom's mind returned to the events in Rome—once again he was surrounded by snipers, and he didn't like the feeling at all.

In the foyer of the concert hall, Father Fjodor, the Patriarch's secretary, came bustling toward them. "President Gennady Vlasov has just arrived," he said, and Hellen's eyes widened. "We were not sure that he would even make it, but now that he is here there will be a brief reception ahead of the official ceremony, just a small gathering. The Patriarch would like to personally show the Cross of Kitezh to the president and the governor of Nizhny Novgorod before presenting it to the wider world. The artifact is of great importance to us Russians."

The man's excitement was palpable and he kept looking around nervously. He took out two VIP passes and handed them to Tom and Hellen.

"The Patriarch would like you to be there. Please follow me."

Without waiting for their reaction, Father Fjodor began to push his way through the waiting crowd.

29

KREMLIN CONCERT HALL, NIZHNY NOVGOROD

They followed the Patriarch's secretary into the empty concert hall, where a cocktail reception had been hastily organized to accompany the presentation of the cross to the visiting luminaries. Around thirty people were already gathered on the stage. The Patriarch was among them—Tom could see him talking with a group of important-looking men. Father Fjodor led Tom and Hellen up a set of stairs and onto the stage, and when the Patriarch saw them his face lit up.

"I am so happy you were able to come! May I introduce the governor of Nizhny Novgorod, Maksim Borislav Nikolayev?" Starting with the governor, Tom and Hellen shook one hand after another as Father Fjodor made the introductions.

"And this is Berlin Brice, a good friend of the governor, and his assistant, Mr. Qadir," Father Fjodor said. "Mr. Brice is an art expert from the United Kingdom."

"From Wales, to be precise," Brice said. His correction did not sound unfriendly or pedantic. There was pride in his voice, in fact.

Tom instantly thought of the first time he met François Cloutard, not that long ago. It had been a similar situation—a famous artifact, a lot of wealthy people—but he did not have a good feeling about Brice at all.

"And you are Hellen de Mey, the famous archeologist," Brice went on, gallantly kissing Hellen's hand. "It's good to see UNESCO making an appearance in this part of the world. Sometimes it seems as if UNESCO rides the coattails of the Americans and goes only where there's oil or other raw materials to be had."

Hellen returned a pained smile. "Blue Shield is active wherever art and history are in danger. Not only in war zones, but also to protect them from grave robbers and smugglers."

Her words carried a double shot of cynicism, and Father Fjodor noticed that the conversation was cooling rapidly. He took the opportunity and said loudly, "Well, it looks as if all of our guests are here. I think we can get started."

It wasn't subtle, but it worked. Tom and Hellen moved away to one side, while those around them talked curiously among themselves, wondering what the spontaneous reception was all about. Around fifty people were now gathered on the concert hall stage.

"Do you know those guys?" Tom asked, nodding back toward Brice and his assistant.

"Yes, I'm sorry to say. People call him 'the Welshman.' He may be an art expert, but he's also a notorious plunderer. Cold-blooded and totally ruthless."

"Like Cloutard, but on the dark side of the Force?"

"That sums him up pretty well, actually."

"So basically, an asshole. We seem to be meeting a lot of those lately," Tom said, and they both chuckled.

A murmur ran through the crowd as all eyes turned to a side door that had just opened. Around twenty-five grim-faced security men in black suits streamed inside and spread out. Everyone knew what that signaled. A few seconds later the Russian president himself entered the concert hall.

"He's even uglier in real life that on TV," Hellen whispered.

"Ms. de Mey, since when are you so rude? Usually it's me who can't keep his opinions to himself."

She poked him in the ribs. "You're a bad influence."

"But you're right," Tom said. "He's no beauty."

Two security guards climbed onto the stage and herded the guests aside to make room for the president, who made his way up the steps behind them.

"Man, the president shows up and they all start pissing their pants," Tom whispered, earning an incensed look from a Russian couple standing close by. The couple bore all the hallmarks of wealthy "New Russians." "Do you suppose they've ever been to Ibiza?" Tom added.

"Hush now!" Hellen hissed.

The mood became more official, and even the "New Russian" stereotypes snapped to attention. The Patriarch, the governor and the president himself each made short speeches, though Tom and Hellen did not understand a word. Then the Patriarch lifted the cross from its velvet-lined case and lifted it high in the air for everyone to see. The guests' faces shone with enthusiasm. The Patriarch presented the cross to the president, pointing toward Tom and Hellen as he did so. They did not understand what was being said, but the Patriarch's words were followed by a vigorous round of applause.

"Looks like we're the heroes of the evening," Tom said, grinning, and he bowed cheerfully. Hellen, however, felt herself blush. She shifted her weight nervously and looked at the floor in embarrassment. To her horror, the Patriarch waved them both over, and she and Tom hesitantly stepped forward. The president handed the cross back to the Patriarch and went to meet them.

"On behalf of the people of Russia, I would like to thank you for coming to help us find our long-lost city," he said. "Спасибо—Spasibo." He shook Hellen's hand, then Tom's.

Without warning, a door on the other side of the hall flew open with a crash.

"The cross will do you no good! Kitezh will soon be lost forever!" shouted a short, non-descript man from the door. He wore a crumpled tweed jacket and his hair was a wild tangle.

Every face turned to the man. The bodyguards with the president stepped protectively between him and the new arrival, their guns trained on the intruder.

"My name is Hillary Graves. I'm a seismologist, and in forty-eight hours an earthquake of magnitude eight or greater is going to devastate everything from Lake Svetloyar to Nizhny Novgorod. Kitezh will sink a second time, and this time forever!"

30

ARTHUR PREY'S APARTMENT, HAVANA, CUBA

"Arthur? May I call you Arthur?" Cloutard said, trying to get Tom's grandfather's attention. "We have to get out of here!"

"You already said that. What do you think we're doing, spring cleaning?" Arthur snapped. "We're packing."

Cloutard grabbed Arthur by the arm and made him look at him. "I mean we have to get out of here *now*. The men looking for you are coming up the stairs *right now!*"

That got Arthur's attention. He paused for a second, then hurried to the front door, locked it and jammed an armchair under the door handle.

Moments later, the two men outside reached the door. They threw their weight against it, but it held.

"They're here," Cloutard whispered into his phone.

Arthur took his revolver from the kitchen table and slipped it into the back of his trousers. He jerked open a drawer and collected several loose bullets, stuffing them in his pocket.

"*Mi vida, vámonos!*" Arthur shouted to Aniel, who had run to the bedroom to get dressed. He took her hand in his and looked deep into her eyes. "Everything will be all right," he said, stroking her hair. "We'll come back for our things later. Now we have to go." Aniel, upset by the commotion, only nodded. Arthur pulled her toward the balcony door. He jerked open the white slatted door and went out first. The two men were still in the hallway, throwing themselves at the apartment door, and the armchair was starting to slip.

"Come on! What are you waiting for?" Arthur shouted back to Cloutard. He followed them out onto the long, slender balcony, which overlooked an alley with two garden restaurants. Cloutard heard music from below and the laughter of patrons. The alley was very narrow and the neighboring building was surrounded by scaffolding for renovation work. They hurried along the balcony to the end.

"We're on the harbor side of the building. Pick us up at the corner," Cloutard shouted into his phone, and hung up.

"We have to get across," Arthur said. He helped Aniel climb over the railing. She jumped and landed neatly on the scaffolding.

"Now you, come on."

"*Mon Dieu,*" Cloutard muttered, looking down. They were only two floors up but even at that altitude he did not like the idea of jumping from one building to another at all, though it was just a few feet. In the meantime, the people in the restaurants had noticed them.

"Go! Hurry!"

Cloutard jumped and found himself a moment later behind the green tarpaulins hanging over the scaffolding. He followed Aniel, who was already climbing down a ladder.

Suddenly, the two thugs charged out onto the balcony. The white curtain billowed through the balcony door behind them. They carried pistols with silencers and looked around wildly. One of them spotted Arthur and fired twice, but the bullets missed Arthur by a hair's breadth as he leaped across to the scaffolding.

The men tucked their pistols into their jeans and took up the chase, jumping across to the scaffolding behind Arthur. But they were too far behind. By the time they had reached the ground and battled their way out through the tarpaulins, all they saw was the red Chevy racing away with its tires squealing. They ran around the building, jumped into their car and sped in pursuit.

"What now? What do we still have to get?" Cloutard said.

"I got to know Artjom Lazarev in Vietnam. He's a Russian Orthodox priest and he saved my life and the life of a young girl there. Years later, he asked me to do him a favor. He gave me an object and asked me to hide it at the other end of the world. I was happy to oblige."

"What was this 'object?'" Cloutard asked.

"I'm afraid I don't really know," Arthur replied. He stepped out of the bushes bordering the gardens of the Castell de la Real Fuerza. Cirilo had driven a few hundred yards, then stopped to let Cloutard and Arthur jump out before driving on with Aniel, luring their pursuers away.

"Do you trust that man?" Arthur asked Cloutard.

"With my life. He will look after your friend, I assure you."

"Then let's go. We have no time to lose." Arthur stepped onto the street and flagged down one of Havana's ubiquitous moped taxis.

"What did you mean when you said you did not know? What is it?" Cloutard asked in surprise.

"It's made of wood, I know that much, and very beautifully crafted. It's like a box, but there's no lid, no opening, no lock," Arthur explained as he climbed into the yellow, egg-shaped taxi. "Come on, get in."

"Into that?" Cloutard shook his head as he stared at the tiny three-wheeled buggy, but he finally climbed inside.

"The perfect vehicle for disappearing in Havana," Arthur said. He turned to the driver and handed him a twenty-dollar bill. "Fábrica de Tabaco Partagas."

31

KREMLIN CONCERT HALL, NIZHNY NOVGOROD

Several of the president's bodyguards had rapidly tackled the hapless man and, despite his loud protests, had dragged him out of the hall. Hellen looked at Tom in shock.

"If that's true, we need to hurry. If an earthquake messes up our plans just before we find Kitezh, I'm going to be very unhappy."

Tom smiled. He liked it when Hellen's passion was stirred. That same spark in her eyes was what had attracted him to her when they had first met, during the Habsburg affair in Vienna. She had been through quite a lot since then, but it had only stoked the fire inside her. Tom could hardly conceal how powerfully attracted to this side of her he was.

"Sure. *If* it's true. We should have a chat with Grillery what's-his-name and see if his story checks out."

Hellen smiled. "'Grillery what's-his-name' is Sir Hillary Graves. He's a famous seismologist."

"Never heard of him."

After the guests vacated the stage, the main doors were opened and the public poured inside. The musicians took their places, and the bells that traditionally announced the start of the concert rang out. The governor, the Patriarch, and the president with his security detail had already disappeared behind the curtains.

"Okay. Let's try and talk to Sir Hillary after the concert. I want to have another word with that Welsh guy, too. I don't like the looks of him," Tom said, feeling inside the pocket of his tuxedo for their tickets. They still had to find their seats. "What are we about to suffer through?"

Hellen waved the program booklet. "A real rarity, but it fits incredibly well. *The Legend of the Invisible City of Kitezh*. It's an opera by Nikolai Rimsky-Korsakov."

"Seriously? There's an opera about it?"

Hellen nodded, unable to hide her smile. She knew how much Tom hated this kind of thing.

"I don't even want to ask, but . . . how long is this going to take? Roughly?" He wobbled his hand in the air.

"About three and a half hours."

"Umm . . . three and a half hours? In Russian?"

"You can do it," Hellen said, patting him encouragingly on the shoulder.

"Remind me to call in a favor from the Patriarch. Three and a half hours of Russian yowling. That's got to be a human rights violation."

They found their seats and the hall fell silent. Then the governor, the Patriarch and the Russian president returned to the stage. The concert hall erupted in whistling and applause.

"I think they're going to reveal the cross to the public," Hellen whispered as the Patriarch began to speak.

"Or maybe they're announcing last week's lotto numbers," Tom said.

Tom noted that Father Fjodor, who rarely left the Patriarch's side, was not with him on stage. Tom turned and scanned the hall in time to see the Patriarch's secretary exiting through one of the side doors. Hellen also noticed his departure. They exchanged a frown.

"Why would the secretary be leaving now?" Hellen asked.

"And why is that bald guy who's sitting with the Welshman and Qadir staring at his watch the whole time?" Tom pointed to where the Welshman sat two rows ahead of them.

"Тихо!" hissed an old lady from the row behind Tom and Hellen.

"I have no idea what that means," Tom whispered, "but I think it's a friendly reminder to pipe down when the dictator speaks."

The Russian president had already launched into a speech. The Patriarch handed him the case that held the cross.

"Everyone seems kind of on edge," Tom whispered as he looked around.

"Yes. They hang on every word he says."

The president had taken the cross out of its case and now held it up proudly for the audience to see. The applause was deafening.

"Kitezh is a big deal for these people," Hellen said. "Almost as big as . . ."

"As the job your mother gave us?" Tom said, finishing her sentence for her. "The one we put on ice for this?" He knew exactly what she was thinking.

"Yes. What Mother showed us is beyond compare. What a sensation for the entire world it would be if we—"

Just then, in the middle of the president's passionate speech, the lights went out and the concert hall was plunged into darkness.

32

FÁBRICA DE TABACO PARTAGAS, HAVANA

The moped taxi pulled up in front of the chestnut-and-cream-colored Fábrica de Tabaco Partagas, situated in an out-of-the-way corner of the Cuban capital, and Cloutard and Arthur climbed out.

"May I ask what we are here for? Provisions?" Cloutard joked as they entered the 175-year-old cigar factory. Immediately to the right was the showroom. Farther back was an atrium with stairs that led up to the production halls, where men and women sat and rolled cigars by hand, day in and day out. These days, evil tongues would call the traditional factory a sweatshop.

In front of the salesroom were wooden benches where a few old men sat and talked in loud voices and puffed on their Havanas. Arthur nodded to one of them, who pointed toward the showroom, and Cloutard followed him inside. They walked straight past the cabinets and shelves filled with the best cigars in the world. At a bar, a handful of tourist slurped mojitos and talked cigars. In a back corner, beside the cash register, was a door labeled "VIP." This was Arthur's destination. When he was close to the cashier, he smiled in greeting, but the old woman abruptly jumped to her feet, pushed past him, and ran straight to Cloutard with her arms in the air.

"Señor Cloutard! We haven't seen you for so long. *Cómo está*?" Arthur was astonished to see the old woman kiss Cloutard on both cheeks in greeting.

"I am well, thank you. Maria, isn't it?"

"*Si señor*," she said, beaming at Cloutard, and she embraced him again. "What can I do for you? The usual?"

Taken aback, Cloutard smiled sheepishly and pointed to Arthur. "We are actually here for him."

She turned to Arthur. "Arthur, *chico malo*, you never told me that you knew François Cloutard," she said, slapping Arthur's rear as if he were a naughty boy. Arthur shrugged and smiled apologetically.

"He is a friend of my grandson. Is your husband here?" Arthur asked the big-hearted woman.

"He's in the back with some friends. Go right in."

Arthur put his arm around Cloutard and guided him toward the VIP room. Cloutard turned back to Maria and said, "Now that I am here, I would take a small box." Maria smiled and nodded.

"Arthur!" cried Ernesto, Maria's husband, followed by a surprised, "And Señor Cloutard?" The door to the VIP room closed behind them. A gray haze hung in the air and an incomparable aroma filled their noses. Ernesto was on his feet and shook both men's hands vigorously. "*Un momento, por favor*," he said. He turned to his four friends, each sitting in a comfortable armchair and enjoying a cigar and a glass of rum, and said, "*Vamonos*. These are important customers." Ernesto's friends grumbled, but they got to their feet and moved toward the door.

Cloutard eyes swept over the countless photographs adorning the walls all around. Politicians, diplomats, crooks and celebrities were immortalized in the pictures, among them Jack Nicholson, Whoopie Goldberg and Gérard Depardieu, to name just a few. Even Hemingway had once been a guest at the cigar bar.

"Good times," Cloutard said nostalgically, and he pointed to one photo in particular. Arthur followed his pointing finger and his eyes widened: Cloutard sat surrounded by soldiers, with none other than Fidel Castro himself at his side. Each of them had a cigar in his mouth and a glass of rum in his hand.

When Ernesto, a chubby man with a thick black moustache, had successfully shooed his friends out of the room, he returned to his newly arrived guests. "I need the casket," said Arthur without hesitation.

Ernesto's smile vanished and he nodded. He went to a corner of the room and pressed on a wooden slat, and a section of wood paneling slid to one side to reveal a secret door. Ernesto opened the narrow door and ducked through it to the room behind, which contained an ancient elevator. Arthur and Cloutard followed. With all three men squeezed into the tiny room, Ernesto closed the wood panel again, and pulled the elevator's accordion gate open. Cloutard's excitement was growing by the second.

"This is really just something neat that we show our VIPs," Ernesto said when he saw Cloutard's enthusiasm. "We only use it when we show important guests around. You know, they look exactly like you did just now." He smiled and pulled the steel gate closed. The cabin gave a jolt and began to rise.

"Why didn't you ever show the elevator to *me*?" Cloutard asked in surprise.

"We only discovered it recently when we were doing renovations. Someone bricked it up years ago," Ernesto explained.

They left the elevator at the production level. The *torcedores*—the men and women who rolled the cigars—sat at antique wooden tables, hidden behind presses and piles of tobacco leaves. This was where they carried out their monotonous work. At the end of the room sat an old woman who read to the *torcedores* from a book while they worked, keeping them entertained. Salsa music seeped quietly from speakers around the room.

The three men crossed the large room. Beside the cargo elevator was the shift supervisor's office, and in one corner of the office stood an almost prehistoric safe, almost six feet tall. Ernesto opened the steel monster and took out a box that, at first glance, might have been mistaken for an ornate humidor. He handed it to Arthur.

"Where else would you keep a box like this?" Arthur said with a smile. "Thank you, my friend," he added, and the three men left the office. They went to the top of the stairs leading down, but suddenly heard a commotion and screams from the bottom of the atrium. They went to the railing and stared down in disbelief.

"*Merde*," Cloutard muttered.

33

KREMLIN CONCERT HALL, NIZHNY NOVGOROD

The only light came from a half dozen exit signs suspended above doorways on each side of the hall. The signs flickered dimly; it was clear that the batteries hadn't been tested in far too long. Frightened cries could be heard, and Tom had the feeling that something was going on. There were people on their feet, moving toward the stage. From his jacket pocket, Tom pulled the small SureFire flashlight he always carried with him. He switched it on.

"Finally, a reason for carrying this thing around all the time," he said to Hellen as the beam of light cut through the darkness. He saw immediately that the bald guy and two more of Brice's men had run up onto the stage. The Russian president had been whisked away by his security detail and was already halfway to the nearest exit. The cross was lying on the stage.

"They're going for the cross!" Tom shouted. He fought his way along the row of seats toward the central aisle.

The bald man—"Cueball" now for Tom—pushed the Patriarch over, picked up the cross and ran from the stage. Tom had reached the central aisle, but many of the concertgoers were on their feet and heading for the exits. Tom had his hands full just fighting against the stream of bodies. There was no way through. He saw that Cueball was pushing his way toward one of the side doors on the right. Just then the lights came back on, and Tom saw that most of the seats between him and the side door were empty.

He vaulted over the first row of seats and was automatically reminded of his high school gym class as he swung himself left and right over the rows. He reached the exit seconds later and ran down a corridor outside the hall. At the end, Cueball was just turning a corner. Tom raced after him and jerked open the door through which the man had disappeared. He found himself in another large hall, where preparations for the banquet set to follow the opera were underway. Waiters were setting places at the tables and getting everything set up for the ceremonial dinner. They looked up as first the bald man, then moments later Tom raced across the hall toward the kitchen.

The automatic door to the kitchen opened whenever anyone approached it and stayed open for several seconds afterward. Tom saw the man collide with one of the kitchen hands, who was mopping the floor. They both went down with a crash, and the air filled with a stream of curses in Russian. Tom seized his chance, and as the man, dripping wet, got up again, Tom threw himself on him.

But his adversary was faster. As he got to his feet, he grabbed the mop and swung it hard at Tom's head. Tom ducked under it and grabbed the kitchen hand's bucket as he straightened, swinging it straight up. The bottom of the iron bucket smashed into Cueball's chin, but the expected reaction did not follow. The man still stood as solid as a rock in front of Tom. He snorted with contempt and grabbed a frying pan. Holding it by the end of its long handle, he swung the pan at high speed at Tom's head. Tom was able to block it with his left arm just in time, but it only softened the impact a little. The force of the blow sent him staggering to the right, where he crashed onto a pile of plates that slipped to the floor and smashed into thousands of pieces. Cueball took advantage of Tom's fall. He turned and ran for the back door.

Tom picked himself up, snatched up a kitchen knife and threw it after the fleeing figure. The knife slashed the man's upper arm, opening a deep wound, before burying itself in the door frame. The man let out a yell and stopped—unfortunately for Tom, right beside a knife block. He turned, and with incredible skill and speed, snatched the various knives out of the block and hurled them at Tom. Tom saw only one escape—he dived head first over the open flames of a massive stove. The knives whistled past and clanged against the pots hanging above it. Then silence. Tom looked out from behind the stove. The kitchen was empty. The staff had fled and Cueball had disappeared.

Tom took off at a run, leaving the kitchen behind. Seconds later found himself at the back entrance of the concert hall. He saw Cueball running toward the main gate of the Kremlin.

You're not getting away from me, buddy, Tom thought, and he took off in pursuit. He dodged through the crowds that filled the kremlin grounds, there to see the fireworks that were the grand finale of the 800th anniversary celebrations. The people of Nizhny Novgorod were not going to miss a show like that. Cueball was not as nimble as Tom and kept crashing into bystanders. Tom was gaining on him rapidly.

But the bald guy had now spotted him, and he changed direction and ran into the Demetrievskaya Tower. He raced up the stairs leading to the broad walkway that topped the wall all the way around the kremlin. Reaching the top of the stairs, Tom saw the man ahead of him, running along the wall. There were no people up here, but Tom still had to deal with obstacles. The walkway was a construction zone—or a garbage dump. Sacks, construction tools, scaffolding and junk were already slowing Cueball down. This was Tom's chance. He had to catch the man and get the cross back, or they would come up, literally, empty-handed.

Cueball stumbled over a fallen ladder and Tom finally caught up with him. He leaped at him, bringing his fist crashing down on the man's skull. Cueball toppled backward, landing on sacks filled with rubble. Tom could smell victory, but he suddenly heard a rumbling noise. He could not tell where it came from. The sound grew louder. Cueball looked up at Tom, his eyes wide—he didn't know what was happening either. Tom realized what it was just before it hit, but he had no time to get to safety. Suddenly, the ground began to tremble and the wall began to crack underneath them.

An earthquake! Sir Hillary was right, Tom thought, looking around desperately for a handhold. But it was too late. A gap opened under his right foot. Tom lost his balance and fell. His right shoulder hit the stone floor hard, and he grimaced in pain. The gap widened, threatening to swallow him. He scrabbled for something, anything he could hold onto and managed to get a grip on part of the workmen's scaffolding. That gave him stability, but only for a second. He fell, and the steel scaffolding came down after him.

34

FÁBRICA DE TABACO PARTAGAS, HAVANA

"Up there!" one of the thugs shouted to his partner, and fired his pistol twice. The two killers they had shaken off earlier with the help of Cloutard's friend were suddenly inside the factory and were already on their way upstairs. Tourists and customers fled in all directions.

"How did they find us?" Arthur said in surprise.

He went for his revolver, but Cloutard stopped him. "It is two guns against one. Besides, there are too many innocent people here who could get hurt."

"You don't happen to have any *real* secret passages out of here, do you?" Arthur asked. Ernesto shook his head.

"Back to the elevator," Cloutard whispered, and all three ran for the antique machine that had carried them up. Cloutard and Arthur climbed inside, but to their surprise Ernesto closed the elevator gate from the outside after pushing the button to send it down.

"Trust me. I have an idea," he said, and he turned back into the room with the *torcedores*. He took off his jacket and shirt and threw them into a corner. Now in only his undershirt, he rubbed grime onto his face and hands. He signaled to his employees to stay calm and keep working. Then he sat at a free table and began to roll a cigar. A moment later, the two killers charged around the corner, pistols drawn.

The men and women, indifferent to the armed men, kept working. They'd all seen worse.

"Where did they go?" one of the men snarled as they marched through the rows looking for Arthur and Cloutard.

Ernesto, in his improvised disguise, said: "Down the back stairs and out the rear entrance." He pointed back toward the cargo elevator. "The elevator takes you straight down to the courtyard."

The men looked at each other, then hurried to the elevator and started down. But as soon as the elevator doors closed, Ernesto jumped to his feet. He ran to the elevator, jerked open the door to the electric panel and switched off the breaker to the elevator, which instantly jolted to a stop between floors. The furious yelling of the two men trapped inside rose through the elevator shaft to the top floor. Ernesto signaled to his people to get downstairs to safety as fast as they could.

Cloutard pulled open the steel gate as soon the antique elevator came to a stop, then opened the secret door that led into the VIP room. He and Arthur rushed out into the salesroom but pulled up short, shocked to find Cirilo waiting for them.

"If I'd known who those two were working for and why they're here, I never would have helped you," he said. He held Arthur's girlfriend by the hair and had a gun pressed to her neck. Ernesto's wife cowered behind the counter, afraid to move an inch.

"Aniel! Let her go, you bastard," Arthur growled.

"I thought we were friends," Cloutard said.

"We are. This has nothing to do with you. You're free to go." He nodded toward the door. "I mean it. Get out of here. All I need is the casket, and I'm sure Mr. Prey here will be happy to part with it in exchange for his girlfriend."

Cloutard looked at Arthur and shrugged indifferently. "*Je suis désolé*. I am sorry," he said, and he stepped cautiously to one side, checking if his friend really meant what he said.

"Go! Disappear!" Cirilo shouted. Cloutard didn't wait to be told a third time. He grabbed his box of cigars, raised his hat in farewell and quickly left the showroom.

"You chickenshit bastard!" Arthur spat after him.

"It seems that honor truly is dead," Cirilo chuckled mockingly.

"Aniel? Are you all right?" Arthur asked.

Aniel nodded, but cried out when Cirilo pulled harder on her hair and pressed the gun harder against her throat. "Put the damned casket on the counter or I'll blow her head off," he said.

Slowly, his free hand raised in surrender, Arthur did as he was told. He set the casket down on top of a glass cabinet and took a few steps back. "You've got what you want. Let her go," he said. He thought of his revolver—all he needed was the right moment. He looked into Aniel's eyes, willing her to understand.

Cirilo pulled the poor woman with him by the hair. When he reached the casket, he held his gun at arm's length, aimed at Arthur.

"I'm sorry, but the people who want this box also want to see you dead."

Now or never, Arthur thought. He was just about to go for his revolver when an ear-splitting noise shattered the tension of the moment. Rubble, dust, cigar boxes and glass flew in all directions as Cirilo's bright red Chevy smashed into the room with terrible force. The crash pushed the cabinets apart and one of them slammed into Cirilo, knocking him over. The casket went flying. Aniel pulled herself free of Cirilo and jumped across to Arthur, who threw a protective arm around her and swung her into cover behind the large column in the center of the showroom.

"What are you waiting for? Get in!" Cloutard shouted. He sat behind the wheel of the convertible, covered in dust but grinning from ear to ear.

"But I need the casket."

"Forget the damned box!" Cloutard shouted at him.

Arthur saw Cirilo, cursing, struggling back onto his feet.

"*Mi amor*, come on," Aniel said, and she tugged at Arthur's arm. Finally, he relented. They both climbed into the car as fast as they could and Cloutard hit the gas. Dust, rubble and shards of glass shot from underneath the spinning wheels, forcing Cirilo to duck for cover. The car tore away down the street, leaving a huge cloud of dust in its wake.

"I thought you'd really bailed on us," Arthur said.

"Are you mad? Do you even know your grandson? He would hunt me to the ends of the earth if anything happened to you while you were you my responsibility," Cloutard said, and he smiled as he turned onto the Malecón and headed for the airport.

35

HOSPITAL ROOM AT THE KREMLIN, NIZHNY NOVGOROD

Tom felt as if someone was jabbing red-hot needles into his eyes. His head was pounding and almost every part of his body hurt. When his eyes had adjusted to the light, he looked around in confusion. He was lying on an examination table in a small hospital room. But that was all that his brain could process, because the next thought that came to him was far worse.

"Shit, they've got the cross!" he said aloud and sat up too quickly, sending a jolt of pain searing through his head.

"No, Tom. They don't." Hellen pressed him gently back onto the bed.

The Patriarch and his secretary, Father Fjodor, entered the room. "Feeling a little better, Mr. Wagner?" the Patriarch asked.

Tom nodded. "I'm all right. My head's exploding, but apart from that . . ." He paused for a moment, then continued, ". . . just scratches. Spoken like a Hollywood action hero, right?"

He grinned at his three visitors. Hellen rolled her eyes, but she was clearly relieved. "There's nothing wrong with him," she said to the Patriarch, who nodded, reassured.

"What about the cross? The bald guy had it and I let him get away. Was that an earthquake? Did Cueball survive? Was anyone else hurt? The earthquake guy was right." Tom slowly sat up again.

"It must be the shock," Hellen said apologetically. "He never talks this much."

"Yes, the earthquake guy was right," Tom heard someone say, and only then did he notice a man sitting in a corner of the room and pressing an ice pack to his head: Sir Hillary himself.

"Looks like being a seismologist didn't help," Tom said with a smile. He pointed to the ice pack. "You still ended up getting bumped on the head."

"This?" Sir Hillary turned his eyes upward and lifted the ice pack for a moment. "This was the president's security guys," he growled. "And yes, a few hours from now all hell is going to break loose. There won't be a building left standing. That earthquake last night was just a little foreshock. According to my calculations, the epicenter will be close to Lake Svetloyar, where the legends say Kitezh is supposed to be."

"If we don't have the cross, we need—"

"But we do have the cross," Father Fjodor interrupted him. All eyes turned to the priest. "I was on my way to the bathroom when the lights went out. A man came running out of the concert hall. He was heading right at me but looking behind him, as if someone was chasing him. I assume that was you." He looked at Tom, who nodded. The priest continued: "He didn't notice me, and all I had to do was stick my leg out. He fell and dropped the cross, and I picked it up. A few seconds later, everyone started coming out of the concert hall and the man ran away."

Tom nodded. "Well, thank God for that. And there I was chasing the wrong guy and nearly breaking my neck." Tom swung his legs over the side of the examination table. "What about the English guy? Brice, wasn't it? He was with Mr. Clean at the concert."

"The Welshman? He disappeared in the chaos," Hellen said as she helped Tom to his feet. He was a little wobbly but already feeling much better.

Tom looked across at Sir Hillary. "I don't know about you, but I need a drink. Fingers crossed they can mix a decent whiskey sour at our hotel. Come and tell us all about our impending Armageddon."

Sir Hillary nodded and they all left the room together. "Gladly, if I can get a single malt. Cocktails made with bourbon are for barbarians."

36

KULIBIN PARK HOTEL, NIZHNY NOVGOROD

"Hellen? You ready? Room service will be here with breakfast any minute." He looked at his watch as he paced back and forth through the living room of their suite. They had separate bedrooms, of course.

"Good," Hellen said as she emerged from her room. "I'm starving." She had pulled on a plain white T-shirt, jeans and New Balance sneakers. She was wearing no makeup at all and had tied her hair back in a practical ponytail.

It was hard for Tom to imagine a simpler outfit, but despite that—or maybe because of it—he found her absolutely captivating. "My stomach's growling, too," he said.

There was a knock at the door, and Tom, playing it safe, spied through the peephole. He raised his eyebrows in surprise.

Hellen interpreted the look correctly. "Not breakfast, I guess," she said. "Who is it?"

Tom did not reply, but simply opened the door.

"Good morning. May I come in?" It was Father Fjodor.

"Of course," Tom said, and stepped aside.

Father Fjodor smiled as he turned to Hellen and bowed his head in greeting. He looked around, taking in the interior of the suite for a moment.

"Please, have a seat," Hellen said, and she gestured toward the small leather easy chairs arranged around the coffee table in the center of the living room.

"I'm sorry to barge in like this without a word of warning, but it's an emergency."

"No problem," Tom said. "What can we do for you?"

"That's something I'd like to discuss elsewhere, if you don't mind," the priest whispered, looking around suspiciously. "Not here. We're in Russia. Walls have ears here."

"But breakfast is on its way," Tom protested, which only earned him a glare from Hellen.

"It's about the cross. I'd prefer to be outside. We can talk safely out there," Father Fjodor said, and he turned toward the door.

"Of course," said Hellen. The cross was more important than breakfast.

Tom sighed. He grabbed the backpack with his laptop inside and followed Hellen and the priest out of the room. The hotel was situated on the edge of Kulibin Park, opposite the Church of the Holy Apostles Peter and Paul. Just past the church, Father Fjodor turned onto a path leading into the park. After a short distance, still looking around cautiously, he spoke again.

"I was afraid they would try to steal it," he said.

"Who are 'they'? And what do you know about the cross that we don't?" Tom said.

"I should have warned you that other, er, individuals are also searching for the invisible city."

"That doesn't surprise me," Hellen said. "The myth of Kitezh has been around for hundreds of years, and people have been searching for it just as long."

Father Fjodor looked down at the ground. "That's true. But the people I'm talking about do not hesitate to kidnap, blackmail and kill to get what they want. They are probably the same ones who tried to steal the cross last night."

"Who are they?" Tom asked.

"I don't know exactly," the priest said. "But I'm certain that they only want the treasures in the invisible city for themselves—and that they would do anything to get them. The mythology and Russia's historical heritage mean nothing to them. Money is all they care about."

Father Fjodor paused for several seconds, as if struggling inwardly. He seemed about to say something else, but stopped himself and said nothing.

"Father, may I ask why you came to us? You obviously know more than you have told us so far," Hellen said. Tom watched the priest intently.

"Stealing the cross makes no sense at all. The cross won't help them find Kitezh. I have no idea why they are even after it," Father Fjodor said, almost to himself.

Tom and Hellen exchanged a suspicious look. The priest knew more about Kitezh than he was saying, that was clear. And Hellen knew Tom well: he did not like it at all if someone tried to lure him down a false trail, let alone into a trap. In Tom's world, withholding information was tantamount to lying, so his reaction came as no great surprise to her.

"With all due respect, Father Fjodor, whatever reasons you might have had not to reveal everything you knew, now's the time to tell us the whole truth. Or we'll be sitting in a plane to Vienna faster than you can say *nostrovia*."

Hellen grinned. Tom, like many others, was unaware that "*nostrovia*" was *not* how the Russians said "cheers." She decided that now was not the time to disabuse him.

"Yes, of course. You've earned the right to know the whole story." Father Fjodor took several deep breaths and closed his eyes before continuing: "It was me who placed the Cross of Kitezh on the Tomb of Saint Peter."

37

SHEREMETEV CASTLE, YURINO

Father Lazarev had reached the limit of his endurance. In the last few hours, various men had screamed at him, beaten him, tortured him. He had had nothing to drink for hours. Sweat and blood covered his aging body. He hurt everywhere. And he could no longer bear the mental pressure they had put him under.

All that kept him alive was the duty he had been entrusted with long ago. That, and the thought that he was not alone in ensuring that the secret of Kitezh would continue to be guarded—because he had taken the precaution of giving the casket to Arthur for safekeeping many years earlier. He could rely on Arthur completely. The casket, he was convinced, was safe somewhere on the other side of the world. It was hardly likely that the men holding him captive had picked up the trail that led to Arthur. Father Lazarev closed his eyes, leaned back and breathed calmly.

Let them kill him. Even if he told them what he knew, it would not get them any further. In itself, the way was only one part of the whole, and they would not be able to bring together the others. Despite the terrible pain wracking his body, Father Lazarev smiled. The legacy of Kitezh would survive.

The door opened and the hairless man, the one who had inflicted most of the pain on him in the last few hours—who even seemed to take pleasure in it—entered the small room. Father Lazarev prayed to God that this would be the end, that he would be freed from his suffering. He knew that he could allow himself to be weak, because he did not need to take his secret with him to the grave.

"Something you are familiar with has come into our possession, old man," the Kahle said.

A dark premonition took root in Father Lazarev's mind. Before he could even ask himself what the man meant, he was holding a cell phone in front of his face. On it was a clear image of the casket. All color drained from the priest's face. He could not keep his emotions under control—sheer horror gripped him.

The man smiled. "It was a coincidence that led us to it. Sadly, fate is not always on the side of you churchmen." He turned around and shouted to someone outside. "Bring him something to eat and drink and patch him up. We need him a little longer. He needs to get his strength back. It looks as if he still has a lot to tell us."

The Kahle's face twisted into a diabolical grin. "No one has ever been able to withstand my methods, and you're not going to be the first, old man. I'll break your will, too." He left the room then, and a few minutes later another man entered, carrying water and a bowl of warm soup. Father Lazarev's heart raced. He was afraid, but his spirit had returned. So it was up to him now, after all. He began to pray. With God's help, he would continue to endure the torture. Suddenly, the old man felt overcome, as if God himself were speaking directly to him. He sensed that this was not the end. He sensed that God would send his angels to help him. He just had to hold on a little longer.

38

KULIBIN PARK, NIZHNY NOVGOROD

Tom and Hellen looked at each other again, this time in surprise.

"Why?" Hellen blurted.

"I did it to get attention," the priest admitted.

"Whose attention?"

"Yours." He looked at Hellen and Tom, his gaze steady. "I have followed your archeological successes in recent years, Ms. de Mey. And your own deeds, Mr. Wagner," he said, turning to Tom, "have not escaped my notice, either. I was convinced that you were the right ones, and—"

"The right ones for what?" Tom said, cutting him off.

The priest ignored his interruption and went on calmly. "God saw to it that you . . ." he nodded toward Tom, ". . . were responsible for the Pope's security. Everything fell into place. I had to act on the spur of the moment."

Hellen was growing impatient. "Please answer the question! For what, exactly, are we the right ones? If everything fell into place, then what for?"

"The city of Kitezh still exists. It is no myth!" Father Fjodor suddenly burst out.

Tom and Hellen were speechless. They first had to digest the priest's revelation. Hellen was the first to find her voice.

"Really? And . . . I mean, I have a thousand questions. Where? How do you know? When can we see it?"

Hellen was suddenly bubbling with enthusiasm. Tom placed a hand on her forearm to try to bring her back down to earth a little. The priest was still holding out on them. There had to be more. Father Fjodor was obviously struggling inwardly.

"Kitezh exists, but only one person knows where it is."

"Who?" Hellen could hardly contain herself. Her cheeks were flushed red. She wanted to know everything then and there.

"My father. Only he knows the way there."

"Your *father*?" Hellen asked in astonishment.

Father Fjodor sighed. "Yes. He is also a priest. And he is the guardian of Kitezh. The guardianship has been in my family for a very long time, passed from generation to generation."

"Wow," Tom said, the best he could manage for now.

"I was overwhelmed when he told me about the guardianship. But he never showed me where it was located or told me about it, and we had a falling out." Sadness filled his eyes. "But if he dies now, the secret dies with him."

"Is he ill?" Hellen asked.

Father Fjodor shook his head.

"Then where is he? Is he in danger?" Tom could already see where this was headed.

"That is one of the reasons I came to you. A few days ago, several armed men forced their way into the church where he usually prays. The bodyguards with him were killed, and he was abducted."

"Do you know who took him?" Tom asked.

"No. But it has to be the same people who tried to steal the cross yesterday."

"The Welshman and his mob. Was this reported to the police?"

"Yes, of course. But it will do no good. We're in Russia. The kidnapping of an old priest is not very high on their agenda, even with the Patriarch's intervention. Besides, I don't trust the police. Whoever kidnapped my father is surely part of the Bratva, or something like it. They will have the police in their pocket."

Tom nodded knowingly.

"This is why I need your help, and I was afraid that I could not simply ask you. The cross was the means to an end, to get you both involved. I beg your forgiveness for that."

Tom's mind was racing. He ran through everyone he could think of who might be behind this.

Hellen looked at him. "You think AF is involved? Noah? Hagen?"

"Hard to say, but I wouldn't be surprised. We have to ask Cloutard. He knows all the players in this particular game," Tom said. He could see that the whole affair had suddenly become a great deal more complicated, especially if the shadowy organization that called itself "Absolute Freedom" was involved. They had completed their circuit through the park and were back at the hotel.

"My father is an old man. He is not as mentally strong as he used to be. We have to hurry. The secret cannot be allowed to fall into the hands of these people, but nor it cannot be lost forever, either. I am sorry I have no more clues to give you," Father Fjodor said.

"Don't worry," Hellen said. We will do everything we can to find your father."

Tom nodded, looking into Hellen's eyes, when an explosion on the third floor of the hotel shattered the morning quiet. All three ducked reflexively. Bits of rubble and glass rained down around them, car alarms wailed, and people ran away screaming. Tom, Hellen and Father Fjodor looked up in dismay. All of them knew immediately which room no longer existed.

"I'm happy to see they didn't just target my apartment," Tom suddenly heard a familiar voice say. He spun around.

"Grandpop!" he cried with relief as he wrapped his arms around the old man.

Hellen greeted Cloutard, who was looking with concern toward the hotel. "Did everything go smoothly?" she asked.

"I would not say 'smoothly,' but we are here and still in one piece," Cloutard replied with a smirk.

The priest was still in shock at the damage done to the hotel. People were streaming out the front door now, and in the distance they could hear the sirens of police cars and fire engines. The rising smoke could no doubt be seen from all over the city.

"Déjà vu," Cloutard murmured.

Tom had recovered from his joy at seeing his grandfather again. "This whole thing is getting uglier and uglier. Exploding apartments and hotel rooms, some mystery man shooting at me, people trying to steal the cross. Who knows what's next?"

Hellen and Cloutard nodded. They knew Tom only too well, and both had seen enough in their recent adventures to know that the moment had come when Tom had had enough.

"Let's get out of here before someone takes it into their head to interrogate us for hours. We need a place where we can talk this through," Tom said, his eyes locked on Father Fjodor.

39

A CHEAP HOTEL IN NIZHNY NOVGOROD

"How are we going to find out where they've taken Father Lazarev?" Hellen asked. Together with Father Fjodor, all four had checked into the first hotel they found. They needed peace and quiet to put together a plan.

"You're a cutting-edge crew, aren't you? Don't you know someone who knows their way around a computer? Push a few buttons and voilà, the information's on your screen like magic," Arthur joked, waving his hands like a conjurer. Father Fjodor smiled.

But Hellen, Cloutard and Tom looked dejectedly at one another.

"*Merde!*" Cloutard swore, upset. It was too soon: the wound was still raw. Noah had been their man for just that kind of thing. But those days were over.

"We're in Russia. Don't hackers practically grow on trees here?" Hellen said, trying to lighten the suddenly dismal mood.

Tom was staring into space, but a hint of a smile played across his face. He stood up and excused himself for a moment.

"Where are you going?" Hellen asked.

But Tom disappeared into the bathroom without a word.

"So, no hacker," Arthur said, and leaned back on his chair.

Ten minutes later, Tom emerged from the bathroom and silently joined the others. He put his laptop on the table in front of him, opened it, and looked around at the others. They exchanged baffled looks, then all eyes finally came to rest on Tom.

"What?" Tom said, surprised to see everyone staring at him.

"What was that just now?" Hellen asked.

"What do you mean?"

"Why all the secretiveness?"

"What secretiveness? I went to the toilet."

Hellen, Arthur and Cloutard were getting annoyed.

"Tom, if you're trying to jerk us around, you're going to have to try harder than that. You didn't even flush!" his grandfather chided.

"Nor did he wash his hands. *Terriblement!*" Cloutard shook his head.

"Tom, we're not back in our big suite here. The walls here are reeeeaaally thin," Hellen added.

He knew he'd been caught. Angry at himself, he tried to salvage what he could.

"I had an idea, and I wanted to follow it up before I said anything and got your hopes up," he said. "If this works out, we'll soon know what happened," he glanced at Father Fjodor, "and where your father ended up."

His friends' mystification only grew.

"And?" Hellen asked.

"What do you mean, 'and'?" Tom didn't want to say any more, but no one was about to let him off the hook. Arthur was practically glaring at his grandson.

"Okay, okay! I got in touch with a guy at the Pentagon, one of my uncle's colleagues, and I asked him to send me satellite images of the area around the lake you told us about," he said, looking at Father Fjodor.

The mystification on the faces around him changed to amazement.

"Just like that?" Hellen asked.

"Uh, yes, just like that," Tom said defensively. "The guy still owed Uncle Scott a favor, and they've been watching Russia very closely from space for a long time. That hasn't changed a bit," he continued. Just then, his email chimed, and he opened the message.

"Let's take a look," he said, clicking on the link in the email. A new window opened.

"Google Earth?" Hellen asked. She decided to keep any more misgivings about Tom's secretiveness to herself for now. At first glance, the window that opened did look like

Google Earth, except that the quality and controls were different.

"Not exactly. When exactly was your father kidnapped?"

"Tuesday night," Father Fjodor said.

Tom's fingers flew over the keyboard, and the results came back instantly. High-resolution satellite recordings in thermal-imaging mode flickered on the monitor. Hellen's, Cloutard's and Arthur's curiosity had been aroused. They were on their feet now and peering over Tom's shoulder.

"That's a terrifying level of detail," Hellen murmured. "Okay, not Google Earth."

The screen showed a forested area surrounding a small lake. Not far from the shore stood a church. The video showed two people in front of the building and one more inside. A car was parked in front of the church.

Suddenly, four more figures, glowing orange, moved into the picture from the edge of the screen, heading toward the church. There was a flash and the two figures stationed at the front of the church fell to the ground. Three of the new arrivals broke into the church. A few seconds later, a van appeared and pulled up out the front.

Father Fjodor sighed and covered his mouth with one hand. Tom realized how painful this must be for the priest and he fast-forwarded a few minutes to spare him the scenes that followed. Before long, the van was driving away.

"We'll find your father," Hellen said, putting one arm reassuringly around the man.

Arthur nodded and said, "My grandson is the best at what he does. He'll get your father back, I'm sure of it."

Tom had now followed the van to its destination and was already doing a little research online.

"You're not going to believe this," he announced after a couple of minutes. Once again, he had their undivided attention.

"*Mon dieu* . . . that is the Welshman!" Cloutard said when he recognized a picture of Berlin Brice on Tom's monitor. "He is the revolting version of me."

"I knew there was a reason he seemed suspicious," Tom said. On the screen was as article about Berlin Brice, a report about how the British businessman had bought the legendary Sheremetev castle in the small town of Yurino, on the banks of the Volga River. According to the official statement, he was planning to renovate the place and restore it to its former glory.

"That's where they're holding your father." Tom pointed to the castle in the background of the picture.

"I know that place," Father Fjodor said. "People call it the 'Pearl of the Volga.' It was built by the Sheremetev family. They were old nobility, relatives of the Romanovs. And if I remember correctly, the previous owner of the castle is buried in the nearby Church of the Archangel Michael."

Tom was studying the satellite images closely. "It looks like the Welshman has a small army stationed there. I count more than fifty men swarming around the place. This is not going to be a picnic."

"We need plans of the estate," Cloutard said.

"There was something in there about renovations, wasn't there? Maybe the plans are in the architect's office?" Tom's grandfather said. He had been standing quietly in the background the whole time.

"Okay, thanks for volunteering. Hellen, you and Grandpop can find the plans," said Tom. His voice had taken on a tone of command that took them all by surprise. "There's just one thing missing. We can't just knock on the front door and tell them we're there to inspect the tapestries." He paused, and his grandfather smiled at him encouragingly. "We need guns. Lots of guns."

"Settle down, Neo," said Cloutard, and he patted Tom placatingly on the shoulder.

Father Fjodor frowned and held up his hands as if surrendering. "I'm a man of God. I can't help you with that."

"But I can," said Cloutard.

"Let me guess," Tom said with a smile. "You know someone who knows someone who earns a not-exactly-legal living buying and selling things that reduce one's life expectancy."

"We are in Russia. Arms trading here is as normal as vodka and borscht." The Frenchman grinned broadly and began to scroll through the contact list on his phone.

40

NIZHNY NOVGOROD

Hellen, Arthur and Father Fjodor sat in their small rental car and looked at the office building across the street. Father Fjodor, who knew the streets of Nizhny Novgorod well and refused to just sit and wait at the hotel, had appointed himself chauffeur. His father's life was on the line, and he wanted to help.

Hellen had done a little online research of her own and, with Father Fjodor's help—Google Translate had been no help at all—had managed to find their destination on the internet. She had discovered that, prior to being bought by the Welshman, the castle had been partly converted to a hotel. Before that, it had stood empty for decades. Even further back in its history, it had served as a hospital in both the First and Second World Wars. A local architectural office had been commissioned to transform the run-down castle into a hotel, but a lack of money and guests had opened the way for a foreign investor on good terms with local corrupt politicians.

Berlin Brice had bought the place for a pittance, and done God only knew what with it since.

After analyzing the satellite images more precisely, Tom had concluded that Brice had surrounded the entire estate with electric fences that traced the route of the old walls.

Hellen's and Arthur's plan was to find the original plans of the castle, in hopes of finding an alternative way to get inside.

"Let's go. Time is pressing," Hellen said, and she climbed out of the car. She and Arthur crossed the street together. Reluctantly, Father Fjodor stayed in the car.

The Mostostroi Architecture and Construction Company had its offices on the top floor of the modest building. As Hellen and Arthur walked from the elevator toward the glass door, it was clear to both of them that they were not in London or New York. The reception area was small and stuffy. The secretary at the reception desk took a long drag on her cigarette and coughed. When she saw Hellen and Arthur approaching, she quickly stubbed out the cigarette and sprayed air freshener around wildly.

"*Dobry den*," the young woman said, forcing a smile.

"Hello. Do you speak English?" Hellen said.

"Yes. How can I help you?" the woman replied with a strong accent.

"My name is Hellen de Mey. I work for Blue Shield, a partner of UNESCO. We would like to speak to one of your engineers, Mr. Mischa Kusnezov. UNESCO is considering adding Sheremetev Castle in Yurino to its list of World Heritage sites. I would like to discuss this with Mr. Kusnezov as soon as possible."

The secretary did her best to take in every word, but Hellen could see that the simultaneous translator in her head was suffering a slight delay. But at the word UNESCO, the woman straightened up a little, and when she saw Hellen's Blue Shield ID, she jumped to her feet.

"Of course. At once! Please have a seat."

"It is very urgent," Hellen said, and she let herself be shooed into the waiting area only with great reluctance. She and Arthur both brusquely turned down the offer of coffee.

"I will be right back!" said the woman, then she excused herself several times and ran down the corridor toward her boss's office at the back of the building.

"We are definitely in Russia," Arthur murmured, looking up at the pictures and plans decorating the walls.

A minute later, the man came hurrying from his office, his assistant circling him like a satellite, plucking and brushing at his suit. As he stuffed his shirt into his trousers and ran his fingers back through his hair, she quickly straightened his tie. Nervous muttering in Russian underscored the surreal scene.

"Good afternoon! Welcome!" said Mischa Kusnezov, shaking Hellen's and Arthur's hands excitedly. "Please come this way." He barked something in Russian to his assistant and she disappeared into the kitchen for refreshments. The engineer ushered Hellen and Arthur toward his office.

41

CHEAP HOTEL IN NIZHNY NOVGOROD

"I have set up a meeting in fifteen minutes."

Tom frowned up at Cloutard. "A meeting? Who with?"

"With someone who can supply us with the necessary equipment. Or did you think they were going to do home delivery for you?" said Cloutard.

"I'm looking forward to this," Tom said as they made their way to the elevator. "Are we going to meet the Russian Cloutard?"

"Not exactly. There can be only one, you know."

"Tell that to the makers of Highlander 2, 3 and 4," Tom shot back.

"Tom, enough of the film trivia, please. We have to think about what we are going to do when we have the necessary equipment. You made a solemn promise to the priest that you would find his father. But if I know you, you have no idea how we are going to do that."

"First things first," Tom replied calmly, waving for a taxi.

Twenty minutes later, the taxi dropped them at an old, dilapidated and deserted-looking farm compound on the outskirts of Nizhny Novgorod. Everything around them looked abandoned. Almost everything . . . Cloutard pointed to the roofline above a gate in the wall surrounding the property. "Camera."

Tom raised one hand to block the glare from the sun. "Shit. I never would have spotted that."

Cloutard approached the left side of the old wooden gate and knocked several times below the bottom hinge. "Good old Morse code," he said.

Tom looked at him in surprise. "You know Morse code?"

Cloutard looked back and raised his eyebrows. "You do not? Amateur! Good help is so hard to find these days."

"Tell me about it," Tom said, grinning. A buzzer sounded and the old wooden gate began to move. "Well, Inspector Clouseau, shall we get back to more important things?"

Tom was already heading through the gate and the yard beyond, where three bizarre-looking vehicles stood. They looked like makeshift hybrids of tank, helicopter, boat and amphibious vehicle, each assembled from a random collection of individual parts. They looked more like sculptures than actual functioning military vehicles, in fact. Only now could Tom and Cloutard see that the yard inside looked very different from the exterior—less like a decaying farm and more like a modern-day army base. A monstrous Rottweiler trotted out of a doorway. It stopped and stared at them, then bared its teeth and barked, although it sounded more like the roar of a bear or lion than the bark of a dog.

"Down, Isidor," a voice said, cutting through the air. The barking stopped, and the dog lay down, the look on its face transforming from threatening to curious.

In the doorway stood a man about forty-five years old, in shorts and a pair of very dark sunglasses, but the most striking thing about him was the garish Hawaiian shirt he wore open to his navel.

"Magnum P.I. called. He wants his clothes back," Tom whispered to Cloutard.

"François!" the man called, then he ran to the Frenchman and threw his arms around him warmly.

"Is there anywhere in the world where you don't have friends?" Tom said, amazed.

"This guy!" the man said, clapping Cloutard on the shoulder. "He saved my life when some nasty KGB boys were about to draw and quarter me."

"You stole their money," Cloutard pointed out.

"No. I borrowed it. I was planning to give it back. One day."

"Tom, I would like you to meet Modest Gagarin," Cloutard said. "And before you ask, no, his father is not named Yuri. Modest, this is Tom Wagner."

Modest nodded. "I've heard quite a bit about you already. Come in, come in!"

Not far away, a black SUV had been standing for several minutes. The Kahle, sitting inside, had watched as Tom and Cloutard got out of their taxi and entered the farmyard.

42
MOSTOSTROI ARCHITECTURE AND CONSTRUCTION COMPANY, NIZHNY NOVGOROD

"Please have a seat," the man said, waving toward two chairs in front of his chaotic desk. "I am very happy that you have come to me for advice. Sheremetev Castle was one of our most ambitious projects. Unfortunately, the investors ran out of money." He held his shoulders excessively straight and his chin raised. "We tried—"

That was as far as he got, because Arthur jammed a stun gun into his neck the moment the door closed behind them. They caught the twitching man as he fell and lowered his unconscious body gently to the floor.

"It was a boring conversation anyway . . . " Arthur said and winked at Hellen. She frowned and tilted her head questioningly. "Star Wars. Han Solo." Arthur rolled his eyes and laughed.

"At least now I know where Tom gets it from. He's always quoting films. But we don't have time for that now. And since we don't have R2 with us, you'll have to use the

Force to find the plans. To work!" Now it was Hellen's turn to smile at him, and Arthur laughed. "You take that plan cabinet, I'll check the computer." She tapped the spacebar to rouse the old PC from sleep. A password field appeared on the screen—in Cyrillic.

"Forget it," she said. "I'm never getting in here."

Despite the minor setback, she turned her attention to a second plan cabinet, sliding the first drawer open as quietly as she could.

"Miss Moneypenny out there could walk in any second with the snacks I'm guessing her boss asked her to get earlier," Arthur said.

"She's an 'executive assistant,'" Hellen said, screwing up her nose at Arthur's unflattering choice of words, as fitting as it might be.

They frantically pulled out one drawer after another, flipping through the various plans and papers inside. Hellen pulled a large folio out of the bottom drawer and laid it on top of the cabinet. She opened it and leafed through the plans.

"I've got something," she whispered.

"Me too."

Arthur came to her and looked at the plans in front of her.

"That's not the castle. I've got that here." He held up several plans rolled together.

"I know, but look at this. These are the original plans from the 19th century." She pointed to a spot on the drawing and her finger followed several lines across the paper.

"Pack it up," said Arthur urgently. "We have to get out of here. We can look at it later."

"Okay, got it." She rolled the plans up and they hurried to the door.

Hellen was already reaching for the handle when the door swung open from outside. The assistant was suddenly standing in the doorway, grinning broadly and balancing a tray of coffee and cookies on one hand. The first things she saw were her boss's legs, sticking out from behind the door. Her smile vanished.

"What is going on here?"

"He was so overwhelmed by the news that he fainted," said Hellen, and she pushed past the woman. The secretary dropped the tray in fright and dashed to her boss's side, screaming and cursing Arthur and Hellen in Russian as they fled. They ignored her and got out of the building as fast as they could.

Father Fjodor started the car as soon as he saw them running from the building. The building's concierge emerged just behind them, shouting, a telephone in his hand, already calling the police.

"What happened?" Father Fjodor asked.

"Hit the gas!" Arthur shouted once he and Hellen were in the car.

"We're a stunning team, literally!" Hellen cried happily as she waved the plans in the air. "And I know how we can get your father out of there!"

43

OUTSKIRTS OF NIZHNY NOVGOROD

As soon as Tom and Cloutard stepped inside the main building, it was clear that the decrepit exterior of the farm was camouflage. The contrast could not have been greater. The room was the size of a small hangar and looked like a cross between an electronics superstore and a junkyard. The tables and shelves were stuffed with technical gear and spare parts spanning decades. Tom saw the open case of an old Commodore 64 lying beside an early LaserDisc player and an Apple Newton. Beside those lay a brand new high-end drone, state-of-the-art night vision gear, VR goggles, and a silver box with "PlayStation 6" on the side.

Farther back, Tom saw a large table holding a ridiculous number of automatic weapons. Some he recognized, others he had never seen before. There was too much stuff lying around in their to take it all in quickly.

"Nice little collection," he said, looked around and grinning with enthusiasm.

"You're probably thinking I must have hacked the accounts of a few Russian oligarchs to put all this together. What can I say? You'd be right." Modest grinned maliciously. "François told me that you need weapons and maybe a few other bits and pieces. He didn't go into detail and, frankly, I don't need to know about it." He turned to Cloutard. "I trust you."

Modest led them past the table of automatic weapons to a door at the end of the hall. He tapped a code into the keypad by the door. There was a beep and the door swung open, and for a few seconds Tom and Cloutard could only stand and gape. The gear inside far exceeded their expectations.

"Impressive!" Tom said. "What do you do with all this stuff?" He was looking at an enormous collection of weapons of every kind, mounted to the walls all around. Like exhibits in a museum, every weapon had a plate beside it with the model name and a few facts about it. Tom saw pistols, revolvers, submachine guns, and sniper rifles from every maker in the trade. Here, too, were several models completely unknown to him.

"It's my hobby. I collect weapons."

"What for?" Tom asked. "The zombie apocalypse?" Even he found this many guns a little suspicious.

"For fun. I just love these things."

"Where did it all come from?"

"After the Soviet Union fell apart, the black market was flooded. You could get almost anything, from atomic missiles to U-boats. Someone else got the U-boat I wanted, unfortunately. It would have been a great toy. No idea who has it now."

"Do you sell, too? Or just collect?"

"Sometimes I sell. Usually to the same people whose accounts I plundered a few months earlier."

Cloutard chuckled knowingly. "Oh, yes. We used to do that all the time."

"A lot of super-rich people are on the lookout for exotic weapons," Modest said. "And they're prepared to pay well for them. The best part is that they mostly just want bragging rights and the weapons never actually get used." He looked at Tom seriously. "I am not some unscrupulous arms dealer, if that's what you think. Go on, help yourself. Take whatever you want."

Tom picked three hand grenades out of a wooden box and began to juggle them, smiling at Cloutard as he did so.

"*Mon ami*, you know weapons are not really my forte."

"Don't be like that. It's not like we're going to war. I just want to have something in my side when the bad guys show up. Just think about Ossana," Tom said.

At the mention of Ossana Ibori, Cloutard nodded eagerly and reached for a Walther PPK. "The gentleman's weapon of choice," he said.

Modest laughed and pointed to a large cupboard on one wall. "Ammunition is in there." He turned to Tom. "Anything else?"

"Yes. We'll need comms," Tom said as he stuffed a silenced FN P90, a silenced Glock, a holster, a bulletproof vest, a knife, and the hand grenades into a black bag.

"So we have to live with you in our ears again?" Cloutard said.

Gagarin led them to one of the many tables back in the hall. Tom's face lit up when he saw the latest AV combat communications gear. "Perfect," he said, adding a few selected pieces to his bag. "We're going to need wheels, too," Tom said, more as a joke. He did not actually believe Modest would have anything like that to offer.

But Modest smiled. "I think I might have just what you need."

Cloutard and Tom looked at each other in surprise and followed the Russian, who pushed open a wooden door at the end of the hall. Tom's heart skipped a beat. In front of him was a brand new Toyota Tundra 6x6 Hercules with all the trimmings.

"Will this do the trick?" Gagarin asked rhetorically.

"Oh, definitely," Tom said.

Modest rummaged in a drawer and took out two keys that he handed to Tom without hesitation.

"The usual rates?" Cloutard asked.

Modest nodded.

Without warning, sirens began to wail, like in sci-fi films when something in the ship goes haywire.

"What the hell is that?" Tom shouted over the din.

"The doorbell," Gagarin said with a laugh. He looked at a bank of monitors. "An old man, a young woman, and . . ." Gagarin's voice faltered for a moment. " . . . a priest?"

"Sounds like the start of a joke, I know, but it's just our friends," Tom said. "We have friend-finder activated, so we always know who's where." Gagarin was not happy at all to hear that. He cherished his anonymity. But friends of Cloutard were friends of his.

A little later, once the introductions had been made, Hellen spread the plans of the castle and the nearby church on one of the large tables and explained to Tom what she had discovered. They studied the plans closely and took another look at the satellite imagery. Then Tom turned to Gagarin.

"Modest, you don't happen to have a helicopter or a light plane, do you?"

"No. But I have something even better," Modest said, wiggling his eyebrows mischievously.

As dusk settled over the old farm, the hulking Toyota Tundra thundered out through the gate. From where he was, the Kahle could not see what had taken place inside the farmyard. He'd been sitting in his parked SUV for hours, out of sight of the entrance, watching. When the Toyota was gone, he climbed out and slowly approached the farm gate. He hammered on it several times with his fist.

44

ORTHODOX CHURCH OF THE ARCHANGEL MICHAEL,
NEAR SHEREMETEV CASTLE, YURINO

Hellen steered the enormous pickup into the narrow side street that led to the north gate of the church. She stopped the car and she, Arthur and Father Fjodor climbed out.

"I'll take care of this. Wait here," said Father Fjodor and he went ahead to the large iron gate. He tugged on the bell pull hanging at the entrance and waited.

It was almost ten in the evening. Father Fjodor rang the bell again. Finally, there was movement inside. A light went on in the house that bordered the property and an old man peered out of a window.

"Who's there?" a hoarse voice asked in Russian. Father Fjodor explained to the old man that the Patriarch of Moscow had sent him. A short while later, locks clicked, the door opened, and the old priest, in his robe, let Father Fjodor inside.

"I'll be right back. This will just take a minute," he said to Hellen and Arthur, and he disappeared into the house.

Outside, the silence was almost complete. In the small town of only 3,500 inhabitants, nothing much happened at that time of night. No cars. No people. They could hear crickets chirping in the grass, and a dog barked now and then. The cloudless sky glittered with stars, and the moonlight doused the night in a mystical, blue-white light. Hellen and Arthur did not talk at first, but after a few minutes of unbroken silence, Arthur said: "So why aren't you two still together?" The question caught Hellen unawares. It was the last thing she was expecting.

"Ummmmm . . ." She was lost for words for several seconds, then finally managed to say, "Arthur, I don't think this is really the right time to talk about Tom's and my love life." She crossed her arms and leaned back against the truck.

"I'll second that," Tom's voice suddenly said on Hellen's headset. She fumbled frantically with the radio and pressed "mute."

"But you were such a great couple," Arthur said. "You were really good for him, and it broke his heart when you went off to work for that old count. I'm happy to see that you've found a way back to each other again."

Hellen gasped. "We're not . . . we haven't . . ." she began, but just then the door of the local priest's house opened and interrupted her attempt to protest. Father Fjodor came out, smiled, and presented them with a heavy old bunch of keys.

"Well, shall we?" said Arthur. He took the keys from Father Fjodor and soon unlocked the heavy iron gate.

Hellen switched on her flashlight, Arthur and Father Fjodor turned on their small LED lamps, and they entered the churchyard.

45

EIGHT THOUSAND FEET ABOVE SHEREMETEV CASTLE, YURINO

Tom had been skeptical when Cloutard's friend had presented this aircraft to them. But his sense of adventure had quickly been aroused, and now he sat beside François eight thousand feet in the air in a little gyrocopter. The McCulloch J-2 was a strange craft, with a special feature that differentiated it from other gyrocopters: the cockpit could seat a pilot and passenger side by side. At first glance, the machine looked like a small helicopter, but from a technical standpoint it was quite different. It could not take off or land vertically, nor could it hover like a normal helicopter. The rotors were not driven directly, but generated enough lift to carry the craft only when the rear-mounted prop gave the aircraft enough forward velocity.

"A little taste?" Cloutard asked, holding a hip flask in front of Tom. Tom shook his head, but the offer made him smile. Cloutard shrugged, then took a long draft from the elegant metal flask.

"Thank God I always have this with me. This rotten little piece of junk does not even have a minibar," Cloutard laughed, and took another mouthful.

"Oh, what the hell," Tom said, and he accepted the flask from Cloutard's hand and took a swallow. "To our anniversary," he added. It was exactly a year since they had both been in a similar situation. The only difference was that, back then, they had been fleeing from Ossana and her henchmen in Tunisia, and they had been in Cloutard's own luxury chopper, which *did* have a minibar. Today, they were sitting in a rusty beast almost sixty years old, in the middle of Russia, on their way to stir up a hornet's nest.

"You have really gone overboard this time, haven't you?" Cloutard said with a quick sideways glance. Tom looked like a modern-day Quasimodo on his way to battle. With the parachute on his back, the bulletproof vest, the silenced P-90 strapped to his chest and the grenades hanging from loops beside it, the magazines stuffed in countless pockets, not to mention the pistol and knife strapped to his thigh, it was difficult for Tom to even sit upright in the tiny cockpit.

"I'll second that," Tom laughed. Cloutard was amazed that Tom actually agreed with him, but Tom shook his head and tapped his headset. "Sorry, Grandpop's interrogating Hellen. You should turn your radio on," he said to Cloutard, who had obviously not heard what Hellen said.

"*Pardonnez-moi*," Cloutard said, immediately correcting the oversight.

"Ha! She's muted it." Tom grinned. "Grandpop was pestering her about why we're not still together."

"Ah. So, why aren't you?"

"Really? You too?" Tom rolled his eyes. "Let's talk about it over a whiskey sour or two, not at eight thousand feet when I'm about to jump out of a flying lawnmower."

"*Assez juste*. But do not think you can worm out of it so easily. One day I expect to hear the full story from both of you."

Tom gave him a pained smile and adjusted his throat mike. Sitting like that was getting increasingly uncomfortable. "Are we there yet?" he asked, sounding for a moment like a kid on a road trip, squirming impatiently in his seat.

"Now do you understand why I miss all my expensive toys?" Cloutard asked.

Tom's headset crackled. He heard Hellen say, "We're in position."

"*En avant!*" Cloutard said.

"Finally," added Tom. He opened the door of the small aircraft and the noise increased exponentially. He turned to his left, ready to jump, but looked back at Cloutard once more. "And to answer your question earlier: No, I haven't gone overboard at all." With a grin, he pulled his goggles over his eyes and dropped into the clear night.

46

ORTHODOX CHURCH OF THE ARCHANGEL MICHAEL,
NEAR SHEREMETEV CASTLE, MINUTES EARLIER

"The crypt of the castle's last owner should be on the south side of the church," Father Fjodor explained.

They made their way past the almost ridiculously quaint, but nevertheless impressive church. Russians considered the red-and-white structure one of their most beautiful Orthodox churches, but it had not always exhibited its present-day splendor. It had been almost destroyed in the 1930s and had then been repurposed, first as a cinema and later as a techno nightclub. Not until the 1990s had it been restored to its original function as a house of God.

On the other side of the church, they quickly found the small fenced-in patch of lawn with the misshapen headstone, topped by an Orthodox cross. The inscription on the headstone was badly eroded and difficult to read. In front of the grave, a narrow stairway led down into the crypt, which lay directly beneath the patch of grass. The narrow stairway looked like the kind leading into those narrow wading basins for cooling off in a sauna, but without the water.

Hellen's excitement grew. She glanced at her watch—they were in good time. They had fifteen minutes to get to the end of the secret passage. She was supposed to meet Tom there, ideally with Father Lazarev.

"Wait here and keep the local priest off our backs, just in case he gets curious," Hellen said to Father Fjodor. She started down the stairs.

Father Fjodor nodded and said, "Don't worry about him."

"And call us on the radio if you see anything suspicious," Arthur added. Father Fjodor nodded again.

Hellen used one of the large keys to open the old iron-clad wooden door and the barred gate behind it while Arthur held his lamp for her to see. The gate swung outward with a creak, and Hellen entered the bare, desolate crypt. The entrance was very low and she had to duck.

"I pictured something more spectacular, actually," Arthur said as he looked around the tiny ten-foot-square room. "The Imperial Crypt in Vienna's in a different league altogether." The ceiling was only about six feet high. A simple rectangular sarcophagus stood against the wall on the left, the Sheremetev family coat of arms in gold relief on the flat, modest lid.

Opposite the entrance was a small white shelf on which a few candles stood, and above the shelf hung an austere-looking cross with a figure of Jesus. Hellen shone her flashlight into every corner of the small chamber, Arthur close behind her.

"That must be it," she said, as the beam of light came to rest on the cross. She stepped closer and examined it carefully. The cross was not simply suspended from a hook, but seemed to be affixed directly to the wall. She shook at it cautiously and tried to turn it. It gave, and she was able to turn it ninety degrees to the left. There was a scraping sound and a click, and dust suddenly trickled from the corner of the ceiling above the cross. The wall had moved a fraction of an inch.

"Help me," she said to Arthur, and they braced themselves against the wall and heaved with all their might. At first with difficulty, and then more easily, they were able to push the wall almost three feet inward.

Out of breath, they paused. Hellen shone her light down what looked like an endless passage to the right. She clicked off the mute button on her headset.

"We're in position."

She took out the pistol Tom had insisted she carry, and she and Arthur entered the dark tunnel leading beneath the castle.

47

FREE FALL OVER SHEREMETEV CASTLE

His last parachute course and his last jump had been a long time ago. But it was like riding a bike—you pull the ripcord and float to the ground. *Piece of cake*, Tom thought. But to minimize the risk of being a sitting duck, he had to wait until the last possible moment to open the chute. Gagarin had explained what kind of parachute it was and at what altitude he had to pull the ripcord. But had he said five hundred feet or eight hundred feet? The Russian's accent had been strong and hard to understand. Five hundred feet—Tom was sure of it. He glanced at the altimeter on his wrist. He was falling at 160 feet per second. Still twenty seconds to go. He hoped that gun-crazy Gagarin had packed the thing properly—if not, there'd be no time for the reserve chute. Tom smiled. This was the kind of buzz that an adrenaline junkie like him lived for—plummeting earthward at more than 120 miles per hour, a smile on his face.

He plunged through a few scraps of cloud, then he saw it directly below in all its glory: Sheremetev Castle. The full moon washed the historic red brick structure and the entire estate in a picturesque, mysterious light. Moonlight was less than ideal for an operation like this, but time was tight and there was no other choice. They had to chance it.

They had studied the plans of the castle and the satellite images carefully. The three-day-old recordings from the satellite feed would have to do.

"What do you mean, your Pentagon 'acquaintance' can't organize a live stream for you? Tom, I'm disappointed," Hellen had teased. After analyzing everything they had, they all agreed that Father Lazarev was most likely being held at the top of the castle tower.

Tom pulled the ripcord and was very happy to see the parachute open exactly as it should. *The crowd goes wild*, he thought as he steered toward the tower, on the southeast side of the building. The landing would not be easy. The tower was only about sixteen feet square from battlement to battlement, and just to complicate things an antenna rose twenty feet into the sky, right in the middle.

The coast looked clear: no guards on the roof. From the satellite images, they knew that most of them were patrolling the high electric fence on the boundary, with a few more on guard at the edge of the forest. No one reckoned with an intruder from above, and Tom and the team had finally decided on a combined assault: Tom by parachute, Hellen and Arthur going through the tunnel Hellen had discovered in the old plans.

Tom landed adroitly behind the battlements, quickly hauling in the parachute the moment it collapsed.

"The Eagle has landed," he joked, his throat mike transmitting his words clearly to the others.

"Nineteen seventy-six. British war film. Michael Caine, Donald Sutherland, Robert Duvall," he heard his grandfather rattle off instantly on the radio.

"You've still got it, Grandpop," said Tom, as he shrugged off the parachute harness and tossed the goggles aside.

"*Je vous demande pardon?*"

"It's a game they play," Hellen explained. "Just ignore them."

Tom focused on the job at hand. With a lockpick, he soon had the door into the tower open.

"Radio silence for now. I'm going in."

With the P-90 raised and ready, Tom carefully opened the door and crept down the steep stairway, which creaked and groaned with every step he took. Ducking below the railing, he followed the stairs along the wall and around a corner, descending into the only room in the tower. He paused on every step and listened. Nothing.

He peered down through the wooden railing into the room below. The moonlight filtering in through three narrow windows cast a feeble glow, and Tom could make out a dark figure on a chair in the center of the room. The creaking of the steps seemed deafening, but nothing moved below. He crept on.

As he drew closer, he could hear the low groans of the priest tied to the chair.

"Father Lazarev?" Tom whispered, approaching the old man cautiously. The priest seemed half-dead already.

"Get away from me. I have nothing more to say to you," Father Lazarev said without looking up, his voice little more than a whisper. His body was slumped forward, and his arms and legs were bound to the chair with cable ties. Blood and sweat dripped from his ravaged face.

"I found the priest. He's alive!" Tom announced on the radio.

"Thank God for that," said Arthur, his relief was almost palpable.

"Father Lazarev," Tom whispered, crouching in front of the man. He lifted the priest's head carefully, and the old man finally opened his eyes and looked at him.

"Aren't you a little young for a killer?" he said.

"My name's Tom Wagner. I'm here to get you out."

"Who are you?"

"I'm here with your son and Arthur Prey."

Spirit and life returned suddenly to the aging, frail body.

"Arthur's alive? He's here?"

"Yes. I'm his grandson, Tom." He sliced through the cable ties binding the priest's arms. Father Lazarev lifted a hand and stroked Tom's cheek.

"Tom," the priest said, with more strength now. "Your grandfather has told me a lot about you."

"All good, I hope," Tom said with a smile as he helped Father Lazarev onto his feet. The old man's strength was gradually returning. Tom's arrival had given him new hope. Suddenly, the old man grasped Tom by the shoulder and looked at him with wide-open eyes.

"The casket! The casket is here! We have to find it."

"What, the casket my grandfather told me—" Tom did not get to finish his question. Voices and footsteps were approaching—someone was climbing the narrow spiral staircase from below. They were trapped.

48

SECRET PASSAGE BETWEEN THE CHURCH OF THE
ARCHANGEL MICHAEL AND SHEREMETEV CASTLE

The passage was low, narrow and rat-infested. Hellen screwed up her face as the damp stench of the tunnel filled her nose. The glare of their lights sent most of the rats scurrying away, but an occasional squeak meant they had stepped on a tail by accident. After about fifty yards, they reached an intersection.

"We have to turn right," Hellen said to Arthur, following close behind. "Then it's two hundred and fifty yards south. That should take us beneath the outbuildings and the ruins of the old wall."

They turned right and followed the passage for a minute in silence. The floor was getting wetter and wetter the closer they got to the castle—and the Volga. Apparently, this part of the tunnel flooded when the river rose high enough.

"So, why—"

But that was as far as Arthur got. Hellen's index finger shot up and she shook her head vehemently, cutting him off. "Grandpop, I'm sorry, but this is neither the time nor the place."

They fell silent again and moved on. Two minutes later, they were directly beneath the gated entrance to the castle. Hellen felt her tension growing. They were approaching the lion's den. A guard could be lurking behind any stone or corner. Hellen checked that the safety on her pistol was off and a round was chambered.

Near the next intersection was a spiral staircase in a corner, leading upward. Hellen shone her flashlight up the stairs—after half a turn it ended at a rusted iron door, secured with a heavy iron chain. "No one's been up or down here for years," she said softly to Arthur.

"That's good," Arthur replied. "That means that probably no one here even knows about these passages."

Hellen nodded and followed the passage onward in the direction of the castle. When they reached the end, they stopped—and she and Arthur exchanged a worried look.

49

SHEREMETEV CASTLE, YURINO

A low *pop, pop—pop, pop* was the only sound the silenced P-90 made. Father Lazarev looked up in horror at the two dead bodies. Moments earlier, Tom had asked the priest to sit down just as he had been when he found him, while Tom himself had taken cover beneath the stairway leading to the roof. From there he could watch the stairs coming up from below. When the two thugs entered the room, one of them flicked on the light. Bare bulbs dangling from the walls illuminated the room, and at the same instant, two shots apiece from the P-90 took the men out. They had no chance at all.

Tom usually avoided going straight for the kill, but there and then he had no other choice. He couldn't risk one of them raising the alarm. Tom returned to Father Lazarev, who looked up at him, appalled at what had just happened.

"Sorry, Father. There was no other way," he whispered. Father Lazarev crossed himself and Tom helped him back to his feet. "We have to go. Your son is waiting outside. We have to get to the cellar without being seen. That's our way out."

"Tom," the priest said, looking at him intently. "We have to find the casket. When they showed it to me, I feared the worst. I thought they'd murdered your grandfather to get it."

"Grandpop's fine. He's down in the cellar as we speak. I'm taking you down to him. The most important thing now is to get you to safety."

The priest nodded and together they made their way slowly down the narrow and seemingly endless spiral staircase from the tower. Tom took the lead, submachine gun at the ready, with Father Lazarev just behind, supporting himself on Tom's shoulder. The old priest was in excellent health for his age, but days of interrogation, torture and sitting had taken their toll, pushing him to his limits. They stopped at the foot of the stairs and Tom looked around.

"The stairs to the cellar are at the end of this corridor," he whispered, pointing to the right. "Can you make it?"

The priest nodded confidently and nudged Tom to go on. Suddenly, a door swung open in front of them, and Tom almost ran into it. He and Father Lazarev froze. Tom slowly lowered the P-90, and when the door swung closed again, he leapt on the back of the man who had just come through it. With a sleeper hold, he sent him silently to dreamland.

Father Lazarev nodded approvingly. He much preferred this method. Tom looked at a sign on the door and pressed his ear against it for a moment. Then he opened it carefully and dragged the man he now recognized as Qadir back into the room he'd just exited.

"Next time, wash your hands after you've been to the bathroom." Tom patted Qadir on the cheek and quickly searched him. All he found was a radio. Tom noted the channel it was switched to, then turned it off. Then he and the priest left the room and hurried along the corridor and down the wide spiral stairway to the cellar. Tom was not expecting to encounter anyone else down there, but suddenly, close to the bottom, they heard a sound.

50

SECRET PASSAGE BENEATH SHEREMETEV CASTLE

Hellen shook the old iron gate, but it would not budge. All she managed to do was rattle the chain. The padlock was rusted solid—there was no way they would be able to pick it. The moisture down there had been eating at the metal for several decades. Short of brute force, Hellen could see no way to get through.

She heard footsteps and shut off her flashlight when she saw a cone of light appear around a corner in the distance. She quickly signaled to Arthur to take cover, and they pressed themselves into niches in the walls on the left and right of the passage. They held their breath. The steps drew closer.

"Tom, where are you?" Hellen whispered into her headset.

"Right here," he said, and Hellen could hardly contain a squeal of delight when she saw him on the other side of the iron gate.

Hellen and Arthur stepped out of the shadows to meet him, a broad grin on his face. Behind him, Father Lazarev stepped into the light.

"Artjom!"

Arthur pressed himself against the gate as the two old friends tried to hug through the bars.

"I feared the worst," Father Lazarev said.

"I'm so sorry. I couldn't protect the casket," said Arthur, sadness in his voice.

"Can we put this reunion on hold for a few minutes?" Tom said as he examined the chain and the iron bars.

"How do you want to open the lock? It's rusted solid," Hellen said. She too had recovered her composure.

Tom took a small glass bottle with a spray top out of his pocket and looked at Hellen in anticipation. "I found this in Gagarin's workshop. I've always wanted to try this stuff. Better step back," he said, and he shooed everyone away from the gate. Then he sprayed the liquid generously onto two links of the chain and put the bottle back in his pocket.

"It's aqua regia," he explained. "Three parts hydrochloric acid to one part nitric acid."

All eyes were now on the chain, which hissed and bubbled and smoked. After a short while, the two links had been eaten away almost completely. Tom struck the chain with the butt of the P-90 and it fell to the floor. Arthur and Father Lazarev could throw their arms around each other at last, and Hellen punched Tom in the ribs.

"Don't ever scare me like that again," she said. Then she hugged him fleetingly and, just as quickly, let go again. Tom herded all of them back into the passage and waved them on. They had to get away from there as fast as they could.

But Father Lazarev would not move. "We still have to get the casket," he said, pointing back up to the castle.

"Why does the casket matter so much? I've been wondering about it ever since you gave it to me," Arthur asked.

"I can't tell you. But it is vital that I get it back," the priest said, his voice deadly serios.

"Does it have to do with Kitezh?" Hellen asked directly, and the priest paled.

"Kit . . . how . . . ?" Words failed him.

"From your son. Long story," Hellen said. The priest's expression darkened, but he nodded in confirmation. "Kitezh is in danger," Hellen continued. "And not just from the men here. In less than 24 hours, an earthquake is going to level the entire area around the lake. And Kitezh, if it even exists, will sink forever."

The last remaining color in Father Lazarev's face now vanished completely. "Oh, it exists, but—"

"Stop!" Tom cut him off. "We're still in the enemy camp. We do *not* have the time to discuss this now. Any second now, they're going to discover that you're AWOL," Tom said, pointing to Father Lazarev, "and then all hell's going to break loose." He urged them forward. But Lazarev would not be moved.

"The casket holds the key to Kitezh," he said. That got their attention. Tom, Hellen and Arthur looked at him in shock. Seconds passed.

"Okay," Tom said. "New plan. You get the hell out of here, fast. I'll get the box." He looked at Father Lazarev. "Where is it?"

"I believe I overheard them say that someone called the Welshman has it," the priest replied.

"Good. Get going. I'll find another way out." Without waiting for an answer, he turned and ran back into the castle.

51

SHEREMETEV CASTLE, YURINO

Tom did not go far. Once his friends had disappeared into the darkness, he switched to the guards' radio channel—and not a second too soon.

"Who the fuck is running around in my castle? Bring the bastard to me!" Berlin Brice's voice bawled in Tom's ear. That could mean only one thing, Tom thought. They'd found the bodies in the tower, and now every available man was looking for him. He had to come up with something, but even as he realized this, he almost ran straight into a guard at the cellar entrance. Just in time, he ducked behind a corner, drew his silenced Glock, and waited.

The man had not seen him. With his back to Tom, he stood and looked around. Tom moved fast. He stepped out of his hiding place and in a low voice commanded, "Gun on the floor, hands in the air, and get on your knees!" The guard did as he was told. Any false move would mean death, he knew, and he wasn't paid well enough for that. Slowly, he laid his machine pistol on the stone floor, laced his fingers behind his head, and lowered himself to his knees.

"Where's Brice keeping the priest's casket?" Tom tapped the back of the man's head with his pistol. "Talk!"

The man squeezed his eyes shut. When he spoke, his voice shook. "I don't know. I'm sorry. I was just doing my rounds."

"Does he have an office or something?"

"Yeah. Second floor. On the right at the top of the stairs."

"How many men are inside?" The guard hesitated, and but Tom gave him another nudge with the barrel of the pistol.

"Five, plus the strange bald guy, the Kahle. The rest are outside. That's all I know. Please don't—" The butt of Tom's Glock sent the man to sleep.

He needed a distraction. He couldn't just wander around the castle and shoot everyone he met. Then a crazy idea occurred to him.

Two minutes later, he ran upstairs to the ground floor, his P-90 at the ready. The castle was mostly dark, with only emergency lamps lighting the corridors. In the lobby, Tom found an open fireplace as tall as he was. His mind returned to Hellen's history lesson about the castle, in particular that there were many of these huge fireplaces in the castle. In one of the salons there was once an extraordinary fireplace, she'd said: two statues, an atlas and a caryatid, had supported the stone mantelpiece surmounting the fireplace, which had been discovered during excavations at Pompeii and moved to the castle.

But during the Soviet era the castle had been plundered; the fireplace was torn out of the wall and carried away. Today, in its place, there was just a roughly-built fireplace lined with tiles from Pompeii.

Tom dashed inside the deep fireplace and waited. Moments later, a massive explosion rocked the castle. The floor shuddered and a cloud of dust billowed up the stairs from the cellar. Two minutes earlier, Tom had placed one of his remaining grenades back at the tunnel entrance. With the help of the aqua regia and the grenade pin, he had improvised a timer. It was enough for a distraction, and the explosion would ideally have been enough to collapse the tunnel entrance, too, preventing anyone from following Hellen and the others. He heard shouting and running feet.

"Go! See what the fuck's going on down there!" The Welshman's bellowing voice rang through the castle. Four men came running from upstairs, straight past Tom and on into the cellar. Tom went the other way, upstairs. At the top, he stopped and peered cautiously around the corner. He saw the Welshman conferring with one of his men. Tom broke cover and—*pop, pop*—the henchman went down. Taken by surprise, but unperturbed, Brice looked down at his blood-spattered suit.

"Where's the casket?" Tom needed no answer. After a question like that, almost everybody's eyes betrayed them. Without fail, they turned toward the hiding place. "Go! In there." Tom jabbed his chin toward the door the Welshman had glanced at.

"Wagner, right?" They moved into Brice's temporary office and Tom quickly looked around.

"Sit. Hands behind your back," Tom ordered, and he tied the Welshman to the chair. The elaborate casket was lying on a plain wooden table.

"You don't seriously think you're going to get out of here alive, do you?"

Tom ignored him. He grabbed a backpack lying in a corner of the room, stowed the box inside it, and slipped his arms through the straps.

"Work with me, Wagner. Let's find the city together. I can make you a rich man, richer than your friend Cloutard ever was."

"You should try shutting the fuck up for a change." Tom plucked the handkerchief from Brice's breast pocket and stuffed it into his mouth. Then he switched the radio back to his friends' channel and left the office.

"François? Come in. I need your help."

Once he'd outlined his plan to Cloutard, he ran up the stairs to the top floor, where he climbed out onto the green-painted metal roof and made his way to the large glass dome that spanned the conservatory. Peering up into the night sky, he failed to notice the Kahle, who had crept onto the roof from the south terrace.

52

SHEREMETEV CASTLE, YURINO

Tom was in trouble. The Kahle had taken him by surprise. Now he had Tom by the throat and was pushing him back against a low wall at his back. Tom had a grip on his hands, which at least was stopping the man from throttling him. Then, in the distance over Baldy's shoulder, Tom saw his way out.

You get crazier ideas every day, he thought. All he had to do was get free for a moment.

He let go of Baldy and smacked him hard on both ears with the palms of his hands. The searing pain caused by the sudden compression in the man's ears gave Tom his opportunity.

Baldy's grip slackened, and with a sharp upward thrust with both arms Tom broke his grip on his throat and kicked him away. The Kahle crashed back hard against the glass dome, and an ugly crack appeared in the glass. Tom snatched a grenade from his vest, pulled the pin and dropped it onto the sloping rooftop. The grenade rolled in the direction of the Kahle, still stunned, who looked first at the roof under his feet and then back at Tom.

"That's for the lives you took in Rome," Tom said, but he could have sworn he saw incomprehension in the man's eyes, as if he had no idea know what Tom was talking about. Tom turned and jumped onto the low wall, then leaped into empty space . . . or not. Because just at that moment, the gyrocopter came roaring over the glass dome and Tom grabbed hold of the rope that Cloutard had tossed out of the cockpit.

The Kahle made a final hopeless attempt to run, but he was too late. The explosion sent him flying back through the glass dome in a blast of lethal shrapnel. He plunged into the depths, landing on the Italian stone floor of the conservatory thirty feet below. His dead eyes stared unmoving into the clear night sky as shards of the dome rained down.

Three hundred yards away, a second hairless man lay atop the roof of an SUV, peering through the sights of a sniper rifle. Just as in Rome, he had Tom in his crosshairs. All he had to do was pull the trigger. He'd already done exactly that more times than he could remember, and not once had he hesitated. Until today.

For the first time in his life, his hand trembled, for he had just watched as Tom took his brother's life.

53

1989, EAST BERLIN

Heinrich was crying bitterly when he and his brother got home from school. The housekeeper, Martha, hugged him and consoled him, only to earn a reproving frown from the boys' father.

"Ignore him, Martha. How are the boys ever supposed to become men if one of them is always blubbering?"

Johann von Falkenhain grabbed little Heinrich by the arm and dragged him into the living room, which was furnished very nicely by East German standards. Heinrich's twin brother, Friedrich, followed silently. He too was close to tears, because he knew what their father had in store for them.

"Before I give you the punishment you seem so sorely to need, I would like to know what happened this time."

Johann was a tall, wiry man with crew-cut hair and a face too lined for his age. He stood as stiff and straight as a soldier on parade and glared disdainfully at his sons, who were no more than an ongoing disappointment for him.

"They made fun of me in school again. They call me ugly because I don't have any hair. They call me 'egghead' and say I look like a monster because I don't have any eyebrows or eyelashes," little Heinrich said, wiping the tears from his eyes.

Friedrich, his own eyes brimming, looked at his brother sympathetically. The two boys were as alike as two eggs. For years, they had suffered mockery and bullying, and at the same time received no support whatsoever from their father, let alone actual love. Their father was a strict and self-righteous man whose harshness had only multiplied after their mother died. Neither of them could remember their mother very well, but they missed the warmth and security she had given them.

Johann looked down at the two boys. Yes, they were freaks. And he could never forgive his dead wife for giving birth to sons like them: sniveling, whiny mama's boys who had nothing of the pride and strength that, for Johann, characterized the typical, German—and yes, Aryan—man. The only hope he saw for change was to punish them, to harden them with pain. One day they would have to stop bawling and develop the kind of manliness sons of his should have.

The two boys instinctively recoiled when they saw their father slip the belt out of his trousers, getting ready to dole out yet another of his innumerable lessons.

But this time, things would be different. Heinrich and Friedrich had talked about it many times, jokingly at first, but then more and more seriously. Friedrich, who at first followed his father's command to turn around, suddenly spun back and screamed at his father: "Leave us alone! We hate you!"

Johann, taken by surprise by his son's reaction, stood as if frozen in place. His lips trembled and he looked down at his son with a mixture of confusion, respect, and disgust.

What he did not notice was that Heinrich had reached into his schoolbag and now held a large carving knife in his hand, stolen from the kitchen days before. Heinrich did not hesitate for a second—he rammed the knife up to the hilt in his father's thigh. His father screamed and fell backward onto the floor. Friedrich, meanwhile, had fetched the hammer from his schoolbag. Like his brother, he was ready to do whatever it took, and one second later, the hammer came down on his father's head. The sound of the splintering skull pierced the boys to their core.

Heinrich had yanked the knife out of his father's leg and now stabbed him in the chest with all his might. Friedrich and Heinrich looked at each other, and from one second to the next the world was a different place. Their determination turned to frenzy. Like wild animals, they beat and stabbed their father, the man who had made their lives a living hell. Until now.

They did not stop for several minutes. Then they looked at each other again, exhausted, and both knew one thing: they had found their calling. Neither needed to say a word to know that what had just happened transcended anything that had ever mattered to them before. No one would ever again make fun of them. No one would ever again persecute them. The tables had turned. The hunted had become the hunters.

"My Lord!" cried Martha, who entered the room just then and saw the blood-covered body of Johann von Falkenhain and, beside him, his two sons, also soaked from head to foot with blood. Seconds later, Martha's life also came to an end.

54

SHEREMETEV CASTLE, YURINO

"Perfect timing!" Tom shouted as he clung to the rope Cloutard had tossed out of the cockpit.

Tom signaled to Cloutard to circle the hole in the castle roof. Below him, he could see the killer's twisted and shrapnel-perforated body. Suddenly, three guards charged out onto the roof and immediately opened fire on the gyrocopter. The bullets missed Tom, but the copter was not as lucky. Several shots struck the engine, which began to sputter and smoke.

Cloutard instantly swung the machine away to the east.

"*Merde!* My friends, we have a little problem," Cloutard said into his radio.

"Don't worry, we can see you," Hellen's voice replied. "We watched your stunt from here and we're on our way."

Behind the small patch of woods that bordered the castle estate was a narrow road that followed the shoreline of the Volga River.

"Look down," Hellen said. Directly beneath Cloutard and Tom, the massive, six-wheeled pickup truck raced along the dusty gravel road. Arthur waved quickly, then pointed behind them.

Tom, still swinging underneath the small aircraft, looked around. Some distance behind, he saw that two black SUVs had taken up the chase. *This is going to be close*, he thought. Tongues of flame were already leaping from the engine cowling and trailing black smoke through the night sky. The old gyrocopter would not be able to stay in the air much longer, that much was clear. And the SUVs were gaining ground quickly.

"We don't have much time. Go lower," Tom shouted to Cloutard, pointing down.

Cloutard brought the sputtering gyrocopter low over the truck. He tried to hold his speed and heading as well as he could, and Tom released the rope, landing hard but safely in the bed of the pickup. The car swerved momentarily as Hellen glanced back over her shoulder. Tom gave her a thumbs up, then drew his pistol and fired at the pursuing SUVs. He waved up to Cloutard.

"Your turn!"

Cloutard shook his head. "Are you insane? How is that supposed to work?" he shouted.

"You open the door and jump," Tom yelled, squeezing off another shot at their pursuers. The bullet hit the windscreen of the leading SUV but simply ricocheted away.

"Bulletproof? Seriously?" Enough messing around. Tom pulled the pin on his last grenade and hurled it at the

SUVs. The blast missed, but one of them, swerving to dodge the grenade, lost control and crashed, rolling over several times.

"One down, one to go," Tom shouted, pleased with his handiwork. "Come on, François, you can do it."

They all had to concentrate now. Hellen drove as straight and steady as she could and Cloutard brought the copter even lower. Tom grabbed the dangling rope and pulled. Then everything happened fast. Cloutard opened the door, hesitated for a moment, and jumped. He knocked Tom over as he landed, and Tom immediately let go of the rope. Hellen pushed the gas pedal to the floor.

Tom and Cloutard looked up in time to admire the spectacle behind them. Like a homing missile, the gyrocopter slammed into the ground in front of the second SUV and burst into flames. The SUV had no time to dodge. It hurtled into the wreckage, and the driver lost control and crashed. The SUV ended up on its roof.

"Nothing but net!" Tom shouted and looked gleefully at Cloutard.

"*Mon Dieu*," Cloutard sighed. "Gagarin is going to kill me. That was a vintage machine, very rare." There were relieved smiles all round as Tom and Cloutard climbed into the cab. Hellen continued along the road beside the river and after another mile she turned north. They passed a house, luxurious-looking for the area, then drove on toward an arm of the Volga. There was no bridge, only a narrow causeway on which the road continued.

"It's about time we—" But Tom did not get to finish his sentence. A tremendous explosion sent the pickup flying.

55

THE WOODS CLOSE TO SHEREMETEV CASTLE

"For Heinrich," he murmured, and squeezed the trigger. The blast from the grenade tore away one of the pickup's rear axles, and the powerful shockwave hurled the truck with Wagner inside end over end before it rolled down the embankment on the far side of the causeway, out of Friedrich's line of sight.

Minutes before, Friedrich had stared as if frozen through the sights of his sniper rifle and witnessed Tom Wagner kill his twin brother.

As often in the past, the two brothers had accepted contracts independent of one another, jobs that took them to the remote corners of the world. Friedrich had not expected at all to find Heinrich here, in the middle of nowhere in Russia. He had been surprised, even briefly amused at the coincidence—and also at the fact that this Tom Wagner probably thought he was fighting him, Friedrich. He had watched the fight for a few moments. It had looked at the start as if his brother was going to win, but the tables had soon turned. Wagner had managed to free himself from Heinrich's grasp and had jumped from the roof. At first, Friedrich hadn't understand what had happened, but then he saw the gyrocopter and the rope with Tom clinging to it.

Through the rifle's sights, he had seen the panic in his brother's eyes. But there was nothing Friedrich could do, and a second later a fireball had engulfed his brother, killing him.

Emotions had welled up inside him in that instant. Fury, disbelief, hatred. Had his hesitation cost his brother his life? What had happened? Wagner had killed Heinrich. And for that he would pay.

Friedrich had watched as the little aircraft roared over his position in the forest before flying alongside the Volga, moving east. He leaped down from the roof of his SUV, threw the sniper rifle on the back seat and raced after the copter. He had driven like a madman through the woods, following a fire trail parallel to the Volga. Wagner had already escaped him twice and surprised him again now, taking out the two SUVs chasing him—the first with a grenade and the second with the gyrocopter itself. Friedrich had to get his hands on the bastard once and for all. Then he would kill him. Slowly. His contract meant little to him now. Wagner had made this personal. He had to die, here and now. So Friedrich, consumed by anger and grief, kept the gas pedal to the floor as he flew along the bumpy fire trail.

Suddenly, he swung the steering wheel hard—lost in thought, he had almost driven straight off the road and into a side arm of the Volga. He turned to the left, trying to stay out of sight of the pickup, and drove alongside the river, keeping one eye on the lights of the pickup with Wagner inside. But the landscape seemed to be trying to thwart him, and the next obstacle in his path soon appeared. The road he was following took another left turn; straight ahead was water. He came to an abrupt halt, picked up the binoculars on the passenger seat, and followed the pickup's progress.

He saw it turn to the northwest. *That brings them back to me*, he thought. With a smile, he put the binoculars aside. He checked the map on his GPS to see where he could cut them off and found the spot he needed just a hundred yards north. Quickly parking his vehicle out of sight behind bushes, he opened the tailgate. In the back lay a second weapons case. He popped it open and lifted out the Colt M4A1, a carbine assault rifle with attached grenade launcher. He grabbed a few spare grenades and a second magazine and found a hiding place not far from the small causeway. All he had to do was wait until the Tundra came down the hill. His grenade sent the SUV crashing into the river.

Friedrich stepped out of his hiding place and walked calmly toward the small river crossing. He slid the spent shell out of the launcher and inserted the new grenade, and also chambered a cartridge in the M4A1. He was taking no chances.

When he reached the crossing, he looked down the embankment. The car lay on its roof about six feet further down, the cab underwater.

Friedrich fired the entire magazine into the car, then switched magazines and emptied the second one into it, too. Then he fired the second grenade, the blast sending water shooting meters into the air. Friedrich squinted as he stared at the burning wreck. Satisfied, he turned around, walked placidly back to his hidden car and drove away.

56

CLOSE TO SHEREMETEV CASTLE

Tom had one hand clamped over Father Fjodor's mouth —the injured priest's cries would have given them all away. Hellen looked into his pain-filled face and did her best to calm him, signaling to him to be quiet. All six were hunched together, bruised and scratched, inside the large drain that passed through the causeway. The water was up to their chests.

When the monstrous and impressively tough Toyota came to rest in the water, they had managed to free themselves just in time and had scrambled into cover inside the drain. The rugged truck was all that had saved their lives. They had barely had time to catch their breath when the deafening sound of automatic gunfire shattered the silence. It was close enough over their heads to make the strongest man cringe in fear, and sheer terror was etched on the faces of Hellen, Cloutard, Arthur, and the two priests. But they were alive. The firing seemed to be over, but then Tom had heard the distinctive click of the grenade launcher barrel locking into place and had thrown himself onto the others, pushing them underwater just as a wall of flame blasted through the tunnel above their submerged heads. But they had dived in time. Father Fjodor, however, had been unfortunate. A chunk of shrapnel had struck him in the side, digging into the flesh between his ribs and hip. Tom, realizing the danger, instantly put his hand over the priest's mouth to muffle his screams.

They had now been sitting for what felt like an eternity inside the stinking pipe. Finally, Tom decided it was time. "I'm going to take my hand off your mouth," he said. "But please, for all our sakes, don't make a sound." Father Fjodor nodded, tears in his eyes. Tom released his grip, and Cloutard and Arthur supported the injured priest. While Hellen checked the others to make sure they were all in one piece, Tom waded slowly to the other end of the pipe.

He climbed the embankment carefully, pistol in hand, and looked around. Apart from a column of black smoke rising into the sky there was nothing to be seen. No one was around. Neither the explosion nor the firing of the automatic weapon seemed to have drawn any attention. He climbed down again and waved to his friends to come out. With difficulty, they managed to get the priest, wracked with pain, up to the road, where they laid him down. Tom inspected the wound and the piece of shrapnel still lodged in his side.

Father Fjodor was close to losing consciousness, but in his delirium he managed to mumble, "Pull it out."

"Don't," Tom said.

"We don't know what might have been injured inside," Hellen explained. "Maybe it's harmless and superficial, but maybe it's more serious. This has to be removed in a hospital, where they can stop the bleeding quickly. The shrapnel is probably stopping you from bleeding to death."

"We can't stay here," said Arthur.

"My son has to get to a hospital," Father Lazarev pleaded.

"We need a vehicle, and we need it now," Cloutard said.

"Agreed," said Tom. "Okay, the rest of you wait here. François and I will find some wheels."

57

DACHA CLOSE TO YURINO, RUSSIA

"We passed some kind of luxury pad just back up the road," Tom said as they jogged up the hill.

"A dacha."

"Gesundheit," Tom said, grinning.

"A 'dacha' is a country house for rich Russians. It is where they go on weekends," Cloutard said, not amused.

Only when they got closer did they see the fence surrounding the entire area. At the large gate, Tom did not hesitate, but immediately rang the bell. Seconds passed and nothing happened. He pressed the bell a second time, then a third, then held his finger on the button for at least thirty seconds. Nothing.

"*Merde*," said Cloutard.

Suddenly, the large gate swung open and a brand new Tesla X rolled almost silently down the driveway. At the wheel sat a young man. When he saw Tom and Cloutard, he stopped and rolled down the window. Tom turned away slightly, keeping his holster out of sight, and Cloutard, pointing to the column of smoke half a mile away, explained in a few words that they'd had an accident and that a priest had been badly hurt.

"Sorry," the driver said. "I can't help you. I've got an appointment to keep that I can't put off for anyone."

He was about to roll the window up again, but Tom's fist was faster. The unconscious driver slumped forward, his head landed on the horn, and the car began to roll forward slowly. Tom jerked the door open, pulled him out, then jumped into the car and stopped it.

"What do we do with him?" Cloutard asked. "Leave him here or take him along?"

"Leave him here," they said in unison. They dragged him to the gate and propped him up against it.

"See if he has a phone," Tom said. "We don't want him calling in the cavalry as soon as he wakes up." Cloutard searched the man's pockets. He found not only a phone but also a pistol: a Jarygin PJa.

"What have we here?" he said. He held the pistol up and Tom raised his eyebrows in surprise—why would the guy be carrying a gun like that? He and Cloutard jumped into the car and drove back to the others.

Hellen had patched up Father Fjodor's injuries as well as she could by the time Tom and Cloutard returned in the stolen Tesla. She had torn strips from the priest's soutane and stabilized the shrapnel. At least now it could not move anymore. But it had been too much for Father Fjodor—he had lost consciousness.

"Perfect," said Hellen when she saw the roomy car. "Help me with him." She opened the gull-wing doors and they laid the injured priest across the center row of seats. Father Lazarev got in on the other side and supported his son's head on his lap. Cloutard took the passenger seat and Arthur and Hellen the third-row seats in the back.

Tom turned around to the back while Cloutard tried to decipher the navigation system. "Sorry it isn't very comfy," he said, "I'll go as fast as I can." Then he turned to the front again and sped away. In a few minutes they reached a larger, paved road and Tom pushed the Tesla to its limits.

"He's going to make it," Arthur said consolingly, placing one hand gently on Artjom's shoulder.

"Thank you, old friend," Father Lazarev said, grasping Arthur's hand. "We have not had the best of relationships in recent years. It has been a long time since we last saw each other. It would be unforgiveable if I were to lose him now." He stroked his son's hair and wiped tears from his own eyes.

"What exactly is your connection with Kitezh?" Hellen asked.

"You frighten me, young lady. But Arthur says I can trust you, and you did save my life. For that, I thank you from the bottom of my heart," Father Lazarev replied. "To answer your question: I am the guardian of Kitezh. The secret of the city has been passed on in my family from generation to generation, father to son. In the casket"—he indicated the box on Cloutard's lap—"is the key."

"If we have the key, then all we need now is the entrance," Hellen said.

"That lies beneath the Church of Our Lady of Kazan, the church of my forefathers, beside Lake Svetloyar. About thirty years ago, I rebuilt it. The place has always been venerated by the faithful, and a church has always stood there," Father Lazarev said.

"How did Kitezh sink in the first place?" Arthur asked.

"An earthquake," the old priest said. "Back when Batu Khan's soldiers were besieging the city. Today, it lies half submerged in an underground lake. Lake Svetloyar is just the tip of the iceberg, so to speak."

"The problem is that this time the quake won't be as kind to Kitezh as the first one was," Tom said. "If that earthquake guy Sir Hillary Graves, is right, it's going to wipe the city out for good."

Father Lazarev sighed. "I know we can't save the entire city. But there is one particular artifact that I have to get to safety. Berlin Brice will stop at nothing to get it, even if it means burying half of Russia."

"What is it?" asked Hellen, looking expectantly at the priest.

"*Ce n'est pas bon*," Cloutard suddenly said.

"What's not good?" Tom asked, glancing across at him.

"My Russian is a little rusty, but unless I'm mistaken, we're sitting in the official car of a Russian general."

"Ah. That would explain why that guy was carrying a military pistol. He was the general's chauffeur, I guess," Tom said.

Cloutard handed a few documents he'd found in the glovebox over to Father Lazarev, who looked through them quickly.

"You're right. General Lubomir Orlovski. The documents are trivial, just order forms for kitchen equipment for the officers' mess." He handed them back to Cloutard.

"Wonderful," Arthur said drily. "You stole a Russian general's car."

"You have to get used to things like this if you spend much time with Tom," Hellen said. "We tend to lurch from one catastrophe to the next."

"Now don't start exaggerating," Tom said. "Everything's under control."

"Unless we happen to bump into the Russian military and the general," Cloutard added, and he took a swig of cognac from his hip flask.

Without warning, Tom slammed on the brakes. The jolt woke Father Fjodor, and he groaned in pain. Tom's hand shot forward. "Fuck, now you've done it," he muttered, and all eyes peered at the soldiers manning a roadblock just ahead of them.

"You were right," Arthur said, looking at Hellen. "From one catastrophe to the next."

Tom rolled slowly toward the roadblock. Father Lazarev opened the back window. A soldier approached and the priest explained their situation to him in Russian. Beside him, his semi-conscious son moaned. After a brief conversation with the solider, Father Lazarev nodded in resignation.

"They have closed off the entire area around Nizhny Novgorod. The authorities have issued an earthquake warning—the whole region is being evacuated. But the soldier says they can escort us to a nearby base. They have an infirmary there where they can treat my son."

"But they won't let us through to Lake Svetloyar, will they?" Hellen asked.

"I'm sorry, no."

"Explain it to him one more time. Maybe if you say the magic word 'Kitezh' he'll turn a blind eye," Tom said, as hopelessly optimistic as ever.

In the meantime, two more soldiers had joined the one at the window and were now eyeing the car suspiciously. One of them reached for his radio.

"I've got a bad feeling about this..." said Tom.

The man with the radio barked an order, and seconds later more than twenty Kalashnikovs were pointing at them.

"I think General Orlovski wants his car back," Tom said. Just as he raised his hands, the earth began to tremble.

58

INTERROGATION ROOM, ARMY BASE NEAR PIGALEVO, RUSSIA

"Why you steal car of general?" the Russian officer screamed.

The soldiers had wasted no time at all. The second foreshock had rattled them, certainly, but no one had been hurt, and the earthquake did not distract the soldiers from the fact that Tom and Cloutard had stolen a very expensive car, belonging to a highly decorated general. They had handcuffed all of them, loaded them onto the back of an old Ural-4320 truck, and driven them to the nearby army base.

On arrival they were immediately separated. Tom suspected that his friends had been taken to the holding cells he'd seen when they'd driven into the base. *I hope they're at least looking after Father Fjodor*, he thought as two soldiers led him, still cuffed, into a windowless room. In the center of the room, a chair stood beneath a dim, dangling light bulb. The floor was spattered with the dried residues of various bodily fluids. The place reeked —the sweaty stench of the soldiers that hauled him onto the chair was the least of it. This was no regular interview room. It was something entirely different, and Tom did not like to think what might have happened in there. In one corner stood a bucket of water with a gray-brown towel slung over it, and Tom suspected it was not there for wiping the floor. Against the wall was a table—in the dim light, Tom could make out various knives and surgical instruments. A ripple of nausea ran through him and his heart began to pound. The steady drip-drip-drip of water from a faucet into the filthy metal washbasin beneath it did not help. Tom's restlessness grew, mixing gradually with a dash of fear.

After what felt like an eternity, the steel door flew open and an officer entered, flanked by two soldiers.

"Who are you? Why you steal car of general?" the officer barked now in broken English, the corners of his mouth pulled down.

"That's a very long story, and I'm afraid we don't have time for long stories. Why don't you call your boss, and he'll call his boss, and so on and so on until you reach President Gennady Vlasov. He'll tell you who I am. If you can't reach him, then—"

The officer stepped toward Tom and backhanded him in the face, hard enough to tip the chair over backward. Tom landed painfully on the cold stone floor.

"No play silly games. Who are you?" the officer shouted again after the two soldiers had set the chair upright.

"Ow!" Tom said loudly and with measured insolence. "You made me bite my tongue." The metallic taste of blood filled his mouth. He spat on the floor in front of the officer. "Ah. That explains all the spots on the floor," he said, and he grinned with bloody teeth at the officer. The officer was ready to hit him a second time, but Tom spoke first: "Okay, seriously. My name is Tom Wagner. I work for Blue Shield. Yeah, I know, who the hell's heard of Blue Shield, right? It kind of belongs to UNESCO. We protect cultural heritage, but whatever. Too complicated. Look, can you at least call the governor of Nizhny Novgorod and the Patriarch of Moscow? They'll clear up everything. The injured man is the Patriarch's private secretary."

The officer said nothing, but stood and pondered things for a moment. Tom could see only the lower half of his grim face. The rest was in shadow.

The officer nodded to one of his soldiers, then turned on his heel and stalked out of the room.

"Hey, where are you going? President Vlasov's waiting for your call," Tom shouted after him. Then the two soldiers stepped in front of him. "Well, boys, what's next?" he said.

59

ARMY BASE NEAR PIGALEVO

Hellen, Cloutard and Father Lazarev walked beside the gurney on which Father Fjodor lay. The soldiers had treated them with undisguised hostility, but they weren't monsters. They could see that Father Fjodor had been seriously wounded—he might have died without Hellen's makeshift stabilization of the injury—and they took him to the infirmary immediately.

"What do we do now?" Arthur whispered, as their military escort led them to the infirmary.

"Tom will find a way to free us and get us to Kitezh," Hellen whispered back confidently.

"And how is he supposed to do that?" Tom's grandfather sounded desperate.

"*Mon ami*, you do not seem to know your grandson very well. Tom is disaster-prone, I admit, but he is also a master at getting out of his disasters. It is as Hellen says: he will find a way."

"Whatever Mr. Wagner does or does not do, I will stay here. I may be the guardian of Kitezh, but I will not leave my son here alone," said Father Lazarev.

The soldiers had removed the old priest's handcuffs—he presented no danger to them—and he held his injured son's hand as he walked beside the gurney.

Hellen nodded. As overjoyed as the scientist in her had been to discover that Kitezh still existed, she could also see that Father Fjodor's life took priority. Cloutard and Arthur, too, had nothing but sympathy for the old priest.

But Father Fjodor, his face contorted in pain, whispered, "You can't do that, Papa. You have to do your duty and get the artifact to safety. Nothing will happen to me here. They will help me, don't worry. You have to go to Kitezh. You know what will happen if the artifact falls into the wrong hands."

The old man's expression darkened. His face suddenly turned stony and a chill entered his voice. "You are right, my son. I have a duty, and I have to see it through," he said. He leaned over and kissed his son on the forehead. They had reached the end of the corridor, and Father Fjodor was pushed into a treatment room.

"This way," they heard a voice from across the corridor, and two soldiers led them into the prison wing, locking them together in one cell.

60

ARMY BASE NEAR PIGALEVO

Tom had no idea how long he'd been out, but it must have been hours. The sky outside was already growing light.

His head throbbed. He sat up with difficulty and leaned back against the wall, drained. He was sitting on a wooden cot in a damp cell with bars on the window and a bucket of water in the corner—*probably more for bodily needs than waterboarding*, he thought. The cell door had a small peephole at eye level and a meal hatch at the level of his waist. He carefully probed the bump on his head left by the butt of a Kalashnikov, then stood up. Still unsteady on his legs, he stumbled to the bucket, sniffed at the contents, then poured the ice-cold water over his head. *Better*, he thought. He could feel his alertness returning.

I need to get out of here fast, he thought. Forces of nature didn't tend to wait for humans or give any consideration at all to their needs.

Tom went to the door and looked out through the peephole. A wooden table stood in front of the cell. The soldier on guard duty sat with his head resting on his crossed arms, snoring loudly. Tom remembered that he'd hidden the little bottle of aqua regia in a secret pocket of his cargo pants, a small compartment sewn to the inside of the right leg, near the cuff. A perfunctory pat-down for weapons was likely to miss something hidden there, and the small bottle was still where he'd put it.

Pity, Tom thought. He would have loved to try breaking out like James Bond did in *Goldfinger*. Tom smiled. He had fond memories of seeing the film for the first time with his grandfather and thinking how cool Sean Connery was as Bond when he tricked the Korean prison guard so cleverly.

But aqua regia would be quicker. Tom lifted the wooden cot and placed it under the barred window, then climbed up. The acid ate mercilessly through the old bars. He was soon able to pull them out easily, and slipped through the window. Unfortunately, he had used up the last of the aqua regia.

The base was silent in the dawn twilight. At one corner of the parade ground, a lamp lit the entrance to the officers' mess, while the spotlight in the guard tower was trained on a fixed point. Tom looked up and saw that the guards in the tower were also sound asleep. *They never would have gotten away with that in the Soviet days*, he thought. Back then, sleeping on duty would earn a soldier a ticket to Siberia, or worse. *Nice to see they're a bit more relaxed about things these days.*

But Tom knew he could not get careless now. Moving close to the wall, he reached the shadows of a porch roof, where he could take a little time to plan his next moves. Number one: a decent set of wheels. Number two: free his friends. Again. He'd done his best to memorize the layout of the base when they first arrived. He crept along beneath the overhanging roof, following the wall of the main building, and glanced cautiously around the corner. Over there was where they kept the vehicles. The rising sun made even the army base look picturesque, and from where he was he could see several UAZ-3151s, the Russian off-road vehicles manufactured by Ulyanovsky Avtomobilny Zavod—the UAZ-3151 was basically the Russian equivalent of a jeep.

Wheels: check.

He waited a few moments, listening, but apart from the rush of the nearby river, he heard nothing. There was no time to waste. The entire camp would be waking up soon. The base was small, just a handful of buildings, so finding their storeroom should not be too difficult, Tom reasoned. And after a few minutes and a few attempts, he found it—along with everything the Russians had taken from them when they were arrested. The only thing missing was the P-90, which had most likely been stolen. The casket, the cross, and even Cloutard's hip flask were all laid out neatly before him.

But that was not all he found. Tom quickly stuffed two military rucksacks with a few uniforms and grabbed two Jarygin PJa pistols and a Kalashnikov, a few boxes of shells, some flares and two army knives. Time was getting away from him and he was forced to take greater risks than he knew were sensible in the situation. He looked up to the guard tower and scanned the parade ground. The coast was still clear. It was now or never. Tom slung the two rucksacks over his shoulder and sprinted across the open ground to where the vehicles were parked. He quickly loosened the straps of one of the vehicles' canvas roof and tossed the rucksacks into the back. Then he went around to the front and checked the winch. He already had a plan for breaking his friends out. If he couldn't break out of prison like Bond, at least he could break his friends out like John Wayne.

61

ARMY BASE NEAR PIGALEVO

First he had to make sure no one would be able to follow them after the breakout, which would not go undiscovered for long. With one of the army knives, Tom slashed the tires of the other vehicles, then stood back and eyed his handiwork. *Discretion is the better part of valor*, he thought. He climbed into the UAZ-3151, pulled the wires out beneath the steering column, and touched them together. The car rumbled to life. He didn't have much time, he knew, and he steered the vehicle toward the small prison tract where he was certain his friends were being held. He pulled up beneath the barred window, jumped out and looked in through the bars. Hellen, Cloutard, Arthur and Father Lazarev were asleep on wooden cots.

"Room service!" Tom said in a loud whisper.

Cloutard was the first on his feet. "*Mon dieu*," he muttered sleepily.

"I know you booked a late checkout, but I'm afraid you'll have to vacate your luxury suite here a little earlier than planned," Tom said as he bent down to the bumper of the UAZ-3151, pulled out the winch hook and wrapped the steel cable around the iron bars. "I saw this in a John Wayne western when I was a kid, and I've wanted to try it ever since."

Grinning broadly, Tom jumped back into the car, backed up carefully until the cable was taut, and floored the gas pedal. At first, the wheels just spun and the winch attachment groaned ominously. Tom eased back on the gas and tried again, this time popping the clutch. The UAZ-3151 jumped backward. The bars held firm in the concrete, but he had succeeded in pulling out half the prison wall, and his four compatriots walked easily out of the cell. Tom freed the hook while the others scrambled into the vehicle.

Jolted awake by the crash, the man in the guard tower stood up too quickly, bashing his head on a beam. When he saw what was happening, he sounded the alarm and seconds later a light came on inside the officers' mess. But Tom and the others were already roaring away in the UAZ-3151. The first shots came from the guard tower, and the sentry at the entrance to the base, startled out of sleep by the noise, was still fumbling with his Kalashnikov when Tom pushed the accelerator to the floor and the car smashed through the boom gate. Seconds later, they were out on the road.

"They'll come after us," Hellen said.

"No they won't," said Tom. "Unless they're as good at swapping out wheels as the pit crews at Monte Carlo."

"Let me guess," said Cloutard. "You slashed their tires."

"*Correctemente*," Tom said.

Cloutard rolled his eyes. "Please, Tom, do not mangle the most beautiful language in the world like that. *Ton prononciation est horrible*."

"Your turn, Father." Tom said, suddenly serious, and he looked Father Lazarev in the eye in the rearview mirror. "Time to come clean. What are we supposed to be saving in Kitezh?"

Hellen's eyes sparkled. Not only was she thankful that Tom had broken them free, she was thrilled that she would soon get to see the invisible city of Kitezh for herself.

Father Lazarev sighed. Everyone turned to him in anticipation.

"Kitezh is not called 'invisible' because it sank and no one could see it anymore. The mythology surrounding the 'invisible' city has a different origin."

Hellen raised her eyebrows. "What do you mean?"

"I'll have to go back a little," the priest began.

"You've got competition," Tom said, smiling mischievously at Hellen. "Let's see if Father Lazarev's history lessons are as gripping as yours." He looked back at the priest. "You should know that whenever Hellen explains something, she has to work through half of human history first."

"Tom, shut up and let the man speak," Arthur chided, growing impatient.

"The city of Kitezh was founded by Yuri II, Grand Prince of Vladimir," Father Lazarev said. "Yuri's lineage traces back to Rurik nobility."

"You mean like the Romanovs, Habsburgs or Babenbergs?" Tom asked.

"Don't forget the Palffys," Cloutard added, nipping at his hip flask.

"Yes, like that," said Father Lazarev. "The Rurikid dynasty ruled Kievan Rus and were the first Tsars of Russia, although the family actually had its roots in Scandinavia. The artifact we have to rescue also has Scandinavian connections."

"Don't tell me we're looking for Thor's hammer! But who would carry it?" Tom's interest was growing.

"You have seen too many films, Tom. Thor's hammer is truly mythological. If it actually existed then it would mean that the gods associated with it also exist," Cloutard said. "My favorite is Loki. Now there's a real crook," he added. He passed the flask to Arthur, who took a swig. The look on Hellen's face spoke volumes. "*C'est suffisant*," said Cloutard, taking the flask back from Arthur—he clearly didn't want to part with too much of his three-thousand-dollar-a-bottle liquor.

"But Thor and Loki don't exist," Hellen said grumpily. "That really is a myth. You might as well tell us we're off to find Siegfried's cloak of invisibility from the Nibelung saga."

Father Lazarev drew a sharp breath and looked at Hellen like a kid caught with his hand in the cookie jar. He did not say a word. Silence settled over the UAZ-3151 for several seconds. Everybody stared at the priest.

"You're kidding," said Hellen in disbelief.

"I assure you I am not. The Rurikids held onto their power because, through their ancestors, they possessed some of the treasures of the Nibelungs. And it's no accident that the fall of Yuri II's branch of the family coincided with the fall of Kitezh." He paused for a moment before continuing emphatically: "These powerful artifacts must never be allowed to fall into the wrong hands. Even if they are buried by the earthquake, the Welshman will never stop looking for them."

Tom nodded. He knew better than any of them what the wrong people could do with powerful tools at their disposal.

"The Nibelung treasure is in Kitezh? *C'est magnifique!*" Cloutard exclaimed.

"Forget it, François. You're not getting any of it for the black market," said Tom.

"If the next words you say are 'it belongs in a museum,' then I will punch you in your face right now," the Frenchman retorted.

"So how exactly do we get to Kitezh?" Tom asked Father Lazarev. "Is there an elevator or something we can take?"

"The first guardian, by pure chance, stumbled onto a cave that led him beneath Lake Svetloyar, where he discovered Kitezh and the secrets that lie hidden there. He wanted to prevent that power from falling into the wrong hands, so he built a church over the cave entrance to keep it concealed and passed the knowledge on to his son. That was the beginning of the guardians of Kitezh."

For the rest of the drive, Hellen was silent. She was going to have to fundamentally reconsider her scientific view of legends and mythology.

62

CHURCH OF OUR LADY OF KAZAN, LAKE SVETLOYAR

"Normally I would not tolerate any kind of weapon in my church, but considering how critical our situation is, I am prepared to make an exception," Father Lazarev said, looking with distaste at the holster strapped to Tom's leg. Just days earlier, the priest had been violently kidnapped from this holy place. He drove the painful memories out of his mind, crossed himself, entered the church and hurried to the altar.

The church was constructed entirely of massive logs and was not particularly big. It was just a rough wooden structure in the middle of nowhere, close to tiny Lake Svetloyar and about a hundred miles from Nizhny Novgorod. Tom and Hellen entered with Father Lazarev and Cloutard and Arthur climbed out of the UAZ-3151 and followed them. They were a strange sight in the Russian army clothes Tom had "borrowed" from the base, and which they had acrobatically pulled on in the jeep on the way to the church.

The church was as plain inside as it was outside. At the altar, Father Lazarev crossed himself again and opened a reliquary, from which he produced a large, ornately bound Bible. Two small locks held the holy book closed. Its cover was pure silver, decorated with elaborate engravings and reliefs. Red gemstones and golden studs had been worked into recesses in the silver.

The priest then lifted out a chain he wore around his neck. On it hung an oval pendant, or locket, about two inches high and engraved with an Orthodox cross, which Father Lazarev opened. Inside was a tiny key. He used the key to unlock the Bible and opened its magnificent cover.

Tom, Hellen, Cloutard and Arthur stood around the altar and watched the clergyman's every dexterous move. Father Lazarev took a goblet from the altar and screwed open its base. A small, coin-like chip fell out. He propped the Bible up and held it open with one hand while the other traced an invisible pattern on the inside cover with the chip.

To their amazement, seven of the walnut-sized golden studs popped out of their recesses in the cover.

"Magnets. Like poles repel one another . . ." said the priest with a smile as he gathered the studs. "Would you place the casket there, please?" he asked Hellen, pointing to an empty space on the altar. Hellen took the elaborately decorated box out of the rucksack and did as the priest asked.

He examined the casket for a moment. For the uninitiated, there was no way to tell which side was the top and which the bottom, and the ornamentation and decorations would not be any help. He picked up the casket and turned it several times, the way one examines a Rubik's cube before starting to turn the sides. Satisfied, he set it down again and placed the metal buttons, one after the other, at strategic points on the five visible sides of the casket. With each one he placed, the box clicked softly—the magnets were definitely moving some kind of mechanism inside. Spellbound, his audience followed every step.

" . . . and opposite poles attract," he said with a theatrical flourish, dropping the final magnet. As if drawn by a magical hand, it fell onto its assigned place. With a loud *clack*, the lid sprang open. Hellen jumped at the sudden noise, surprised and delighted, although she had expected nothing less. She beamed at Tom, who seemed as fascinated as she was.

"Cool," he whispered.

Cloutard and Arthur nodded appreciatively. Inside the casket were two metal plates, each about four inches long, an inch across, and an eighth of an inch thick.

"The cross, please." Without a word, Tom handed over the cross he had found just a few days before at the Tomb of St. Peter.

In contrast to the Roman Catholic cross, a Russian, Orthodox or Byzantine cross has not one but three crossbeams. The uppermost beam symbolizes the board on which "INRI"— the Latin abbreviation for "Jesus of Nazareth, King of the Jews"—was inscribed, while the lowest beam, set at an angle, represents the plank supporting his feet. Father Lazarev now added the two metal plates to the lower section of the cross. They clicked into place almost silently.

"Finished," he said, presenting the newly created object.

"With a little imagination it could pass for an oversized key," Tom said.

"As I said: the casket holds the key to Kitezh."

"And where's the lock that it fits?" Hellen asked, unable to contain her curiosity.

"Come with me."

The priest led them to the center of the church. A roughly circular relief, consisting of seven triangles, had been worked into the plain stone floor, each of its seven segments covered in metal. If not for the beautiful ornamentation, representing the seven days of the Christian creation, and the fact that it was set into the floor of a church, it could easily have been mistaken for a fancy manhole cover. More than six feet across, the seven-cornered relief had a small circular cover at its center. Father Lazarev removed this and inserted the long end of the cross into the opening. He turned it counter-clockwise and, creaking all the way, the seven triangular segments swung slowly upwards and outwards. Underneath was a circular, brick-lined shaft five feet in diameter. An iron spiral staircase wound into the depths.

"How strong are those steps?" Tom asked. "We had a little mishap a year back and—" Hellen shook her head and elbowed Tom in the ribs, and he instantly shut up.

"Don't worry. It's perfectly safe," Father Lazarev assured him.

Suddenly, Cloutard pricked up his ears. "A car is coming," he warned. He ran to the front of the church and bolted the front door.

"Hurry," said Father Lazarev, removing the cross. He put it away in a pocket of his army overalls, zipping it closed.

One after the other, the five quickly made their way down the spiral staircase. Father Lazarev was the last to descend and with the help of a rusty handle set in a hollow in the wall, he closed the entrance again. There was no turning back now.

63

CHURCH OF OUR LADY OF KAZAN, LAKE SVETLOYAR

Wood splintered as the church door crashed open. Dust drifted down from from the ceiling, shimmering in the harsh light of the morning sun flooding through the windows. Berlin Brice stepped inside, followed closely by his right-hand man, Qadir, and four Russian soldiers. The soldiers, not especially faithful to the chain of command, were moonlighting with the Welshman to supplement their meager salaries. Brice had informants everywhere, even in the Russian military—it was they who had informed him that Wagner and his people had been arrested. Unfortunately, he'd arrived too late. Tom Wagner had already flown the coop.

"Find the entrance. It has to be here somewhere." The four men nodded obediently and scurried off to search every corner of the church. In the meantime, Brice approached the altar. The first thing that caught his eye was the impressive Bible. He picked it up and turned a few pages.

"You've done some first-class work here, old man," he whispered, impressed, as his fingers glided over the recesses in the cover. He put the Bible aside and his gaze moved over the altar until he saw the open casket. It was empty.

"And Wagner? Whose brilliant idea was it to bring fucking Tom Wagner into this?" he said through clenched teeth, his fingers clawing at the ancient wood.

"Sir?" Qadir asked in confusion.

"It was a rhetorical question." In a rage, Brice threw the casket back onto the altar—too hard, knocking everything onto the floor.

He turned around and stalked back toward the entrance. Halfway there, he suddenly froze and looked down. He was standing at the center of an ornamental relief more than six feet across, depicting the seven days of Creation. He crouched and rain his fingers along the edges of the metal frame that separated the panels.

"I've found it, you good-for-nothing idiots." He straightened up and stamped his feet on the floor. The four soldiers hurried over.

"Here! Open it!"

One of the men immediately ran outside and returned a moment later with a tire iron, with which he set to work on the embedded metal frame. But his efforts were futile. The metal construction had been built too precisely, not even the tire iron would fit.

"Am I surrounded by morons?" Brice bawled, snatching the tire iron from the man's hands and throwing it aside.

He snatched one of the hand grenades dangling from the man's tactical vest, pulled the pin and pressed the grenade back in the bewildered man's hand. He clapped him on the shoulder and walked outside calmly with Qadir.

"Whenever you're ready, soldier," he shouted back as he disappeared out the door. Seconds later the grenade exploded, just as the last of the soldiers charged out through the door to safety. When the dust had settled, Brice went back inside. The seven-paneled relief had been reduced to twisted metal and a gaping hole in the floor. He stared down into the shaft, satisfied.

"The gateway to Kitezh," he sighed, awestruck. He'd had his doubts about whether he would ever get to see this fabled place. The four soldiers, not looking happy at all, came back inside, dusting off their uniforms.

"Right, get down there!" Brice ordered. The soldiers just looked at him less than enthusiastically.

"But . . . the earthquake?" one said, earning an angry, intimidating glare from the Welshman. After a moment's hesitation they followed the order—he was the money man, after all—and began to descend the stairs. The staircase was very narrow, and at the start the soldiers had trouble getting down it with their AK-47s.

"I want that treasure in my hands today," Brice said. He followed the soldiers down, with Qadir bringing up the rear.

64

BENEATH THE CHURCH OF OUR LADY OF KAZAN, LAKE SVETLOYAR

It took a long time, but they finally reached the bottom of the winding stairs, where they found themselves in a sloping hall the size of the center court at Wimbledon, but with considerably less headroom. Suddenly, they heard a thundering roar overhead and the stairway vibrated loudly. Their first thought was another quake, and Tom and Hellen swung their flashlights toward the stairs.

"That was no tremor," said Tom, pointing back up the way they'd come. "That was an explosion. Brice is in a hell of a hurry."

"*La vache!*" Cloutard took off his cap and ran his fingers through his hair. Climbing down the stairs had already taken him out of his comfort zone.

"Then we'd better pick up the pace ourselves," said Arthur.

"How far is it?" Hellen asked.

"We are almost there, my dear," Father Lazarev assured her, and he pointed toward a V-shaped passage between walls of rock. Hellen shone her light in the direction he indicated. "And you won't be needing those anymore," he added, nodding toward Hellen's flashlight. "It took my father and me more than a year," he said, flicking a switch in an old electrical cabinet next to the stairs, "just to install these lights."

When the lights came on, the four newcomers looked around in amazement. Cables were strung like garlands along the walls. A bulb shone every ten yards, in a string that disappeared down the passageway.

"As a young man, I swore that for as long as I lived, I would explore every inch of this underground wonderland, and I was not going to do it with a lamp strapped to my head," Father Lazarev said with a chuckle.

Tom and Hellen switched off their flashlights.

"I hear footsteps. They're on their way. We have to move," Tom said urgently.

"This way." Father Lazarev took the lead into the narrow passage, following the lights. The priest and his father had not only installed the lights; they had also wedged wooden planks where the rock walls came together at the bottom of the V. Slowly, the team balanced their along the planks through the gap in the rock.

"What's that?" Hellen looked up in surprise.

"What's what?" Tom asked, close behind her.

"That sound." She snapped on her flashlight again and shone it up into the high passageway. Something moved in the shadows.

"Wow! Look at that!" Hellen cried in amazement as she gazed up at hundreds of bats hanging from the ceiling.

"*Mon dieu*, all this tomb raiding is not for me," said Cloutard, shaking his head in disgust and walking faster. "This is why I always stuck to management."

"Watch out you don't get one in your hair," Tom said to Hellen with a laugh, and she smiled as he tousled her hair.

But then his grin vanished. The hairs on the back of his neck stood on end, and in the same instant he heard the sound of the bolt being racked on an AK-47.

"Run!" Sparks flew as a hail of bullets struck the rocks around them. They were lucky not to be hit by a ricochet. Ducking low, hands over their heads, they ran on as fast as they could. As they ran, they heard the fluttering of wings and the squeals of hundreds of bats dropping from the ceiling and flying away above their heads.

"Keep going," Tom shouted, waving his friends onward. "I'll try to stop them."

Russian curses and the sound of gunfire reverberated along the passage as the swarm of bats reached the pursuing soldiers. For Tom, the bats created a welcome diversion. Looking up at the ceiling, he had an idea. He ducked into a dark cleft for a moment until he saw the first soldier coming. Tom fired and the man went down. Then he aimed his pistol upward and emptied the entire magazine. It worked: an avalanche of stone broke loose, tumbling down on top of the fallen soldier, burying him and blocking the passageway with a good six feet of rubble.

That should keep them busy for a while, Tom thought, as he turned and hurried after his friends. Behind him he heard the shouting and cursing of Berlin Brice. Moments later, when Tom stepped out of the passage, his jaw almost hit the floor.

65

BENEATH THE CHURCH OF OUR LADY OF KAZAN, LAKE SVETLOYAR

Tom had stepped into another world. Open-mouthed and silent, Hellen, Cloutard and Arthur were standing on the shore of an enormous subterranean lake, staring into a seemingly endless cave.

"Oh. *Mon dieu*. This must be what Otto Lidenbrock felt like."

"Gollum would feel right at home here," said Arthur.

"The perfect place to hide a Horcrux," Hellen whispered.

"All that's missing is Nazis riding dinosaurs," said Tom, joining his friends.

Father Lazarev smiled. When his father had brought him down here for the first time, his own reaction had been similar. Now, however, he felt a tinge of sadness—all of it might soon be destroyed for good, and he would never again see this magical place.

The roof of the magnificent cave, created by the last earthquake 800 years earlier, hung suspended about thirty feet over the surface of the lake, which was many times larger than Lake Svetloyar, far above their heads.

They first had to digest the knowledge that they were standing several stories below the bed of little Lake Svetloyar. Only then was it possible to appreciate the next wonder: far out on the gigantic lake rose the top section of a tower, crowned by a gleaming, golden onion dome.

"Ow!" Hellen cried. Tom had pinched her arm.

"Just checking," he said cheekily.

She rubbed the spot he'd pinched and turned to Father Lazarev. "How did you . . . how is it . . ." She was so overcome that she could not even finish a sentence. Influenced by her father, Hellen had grown up around archeology and had become an authority of some renown herself. But this place completely undid her understanding of what her profession meant. This place shouldn't exist—and yet here it was.

Father Lazarev was overjoyed to be able to share his secret with someone else at last, if only for a few final hours.

"Do you know what this means?" Hellen said to Tom, Arthur and François, who were still gazing out over the lake. All three answered with a simple shake of their heads. "If this place actually exists, a place that people out there think of as no more than an exciting bedtime story, then there must be countless other secrets and myths just like this one, waiting to be discovered.

"So what do we do now?" Cloutard asked.

"We have to row over there with the boat," Father Lazarev said, pointing out to the tower. "At the foot of the tower there is a chest. Inside we'll find Siegfried's cloak and the sword with which he is said to have slain the dragon."

For a moment, they had forgotten the bloody-minded mercenaries at their heels. But they had another, far more dangerous enemy, which made its presence felt just then with a merciless display of power: once again, the earth trembled. Tom and his companions had trouble staying on their feet, and boulders crashed from the ceiling.

"Come on. To find the treasure we have to get out to the tower." Father Lazarev waved the others to follow him. Arthur, who was closest, immediately trotted ahead into a passage that Father Lazarev pointed him toward, the priest close behind him.

"Hurry," the priest called. Tom, Hellen and Cloutard began making their way around a large boulder, but before they reached the passage Father Lazarev cried "Stop! It's going to collapse!"

"Grandpop!" Tom shouted. Looking ahead, he saw only his grandfather's fear-filled face. Cloutard had to hold Tom back as dust, sand and small stones began raining down.

"Blessed are the pure of heart, for they shall see the truth," Father Lazarev called, looking intently at Hellen.

In a rumble of rock and dust, the narrow passage collapsed, burying Father Lazarev and Tom's grandfather.

"*Grandpop!!*" Tom cried in horror. He pushed past Cloutard and began clawing at the stones that had fallen from the cave roof, but Cloutard pulled him back just in time, as a second rockfall came crashing down.

As quickly as it had begun, the foreshock came to an end. Tom struggled to break free of Cloutard's and Hellen's grip. Tears flooded his eyes and he sank to his knees on the cave floor, overcome with grief. After his parents had been murdered, Arthur had raised him. He had become more like a father than a grandfather to Tom, and more: he was the best friend Tom had. Hellen stepped forward and laid a consoling hand on his cheek.

"Tom. Tom, we don't know what happened. Maybe they made it. We don't know how far along the passage collapsed. Father Lazarev is sure to know another way out."

Tom nodded, still distraught. He wiped his eyes and struggled to calm down.

"We should get out of here as quickly as we can," Cloutard said.

"No!" Tom said, his voice like iron as he got to his feet. "If my grandfather is dead, he cannot have died in vain. We're going to get that damned cloak if it's the last thing we do."

"You took the words right out of my mouth," they suddenly heard Berlin Brice say. The Welshman stepped out of the main passage with a .22-caliber revolver in his hand.

"Drop your gun!" Qadir snapped, appearing from the passage right behind Brice with the three remaining soldiers. Tom could see they had no chance. He laid his pistol on the floor and kicked it aside. He, Hellen and Cloutard raised their hands.

"What's become of Father Lazarev and your grandfather?" Brice asked. He got no answer, but none was necessary. He could see it in their faces. "My sincere condolences. All I wanted was the cloak and to finally get to see this incredible place. No one had to get hurt or die. But that selfish guardian wanted to keep it all for himself and no one else. He wanted to hide it away from the world."

"That's because the world isn't ready for a power like—" Hellen began, but Tom cut her off.

"Hellen, don't make this sociopath any angrier than he already is." Tom had leaned close to Hellen as if to whisper in her ear, but had spoken loudly enough for everyone to hear what he said.

"You must think you're a funny guy, don't you?" Brice said, and he nodded almost imperceptibly toward Qadir. Qadir stepped forward and slammed his fist into Tom's stomach with all his strength. Tom fell to his knees, gasping for air.

"Tom!" Hellen cried. She lowered her hands and went to help him up, but the sight of Qadir's Kalashnikov in her face changed her mind.

"Well, then," Brice said, pacing back and forth in front of them. "Shall we move on to the uncomfortable part?

Where do we go from here? I have no doubt the good padre told you where to find the cloak."

Hellen and Cloutard said nothing. Tom was struggling to get back onto his feet. "It's hidden up your ass," he said, but broke down coughing and dropped to his knees again, unable to catch his breath.

"Wait!" Hellen pleaded, positioning herself between Tom and Qadir.

"Hellen, no," Tom wheezed. "Don't tell him anything."

"We have to take the boat," Hellen began, pointing to the little dinghy tied up at the shore of the lake, "and row out to the tower."

"Then what are we waiting for?" Brice said, waving Hellen and Tom down toward the shore. "Stay here and watch the Frenchman," he said to Qadir. Hellen and Tom climbed into the boat, followed by one of the soldiers. Brice pushed the boat away from the shore and climbed in after them.

66

KITEZH CHURCH TOWER, BENEATH LAKE SVETLOYAR

"What are you doing?" Brice asked as Hellen took a flare out of her rucksack.

"I want to take a look down below, that's all."

Brice's eyes flicked from Hellen to the flare, then to the surface of the lake. He nodded, signaling with his little revolver that Hellen should throw the flare into the dark water, where it sank slowly toward the lakebed. The water was crystal clear and seemed almost bottomless. Hellen tossed a second flare after the first one and she and Brice gazed eagerly into the depths. The fiery light allowed them to see at least a little of what lay hidden beneath the surface, enormous structures appearing hazily in the flickering red-orange of the flares. The ruins seemed to go on forever, and some of the remains looked remarkably intact. *An explorer could spend months diving here without seeing everything*, Hellen thought.

For a moment, she forgot that she and Tom were on the wrong side of an AK-47. The young soldier holding it would obviously have liked to risk a glance over the side, but he kept his focus on Tom.

Hellen was both thrilled and deeply saddened. All of what she was looking at would soon be gone forever. And if she knew that if she ever told anyone about it, they would not believe her.

Cracking and grinding echoed through the endless cave. The rock seemed to be alive. Her and there, chunks broke free and plunged into the lake. Water from Lake Svetloyar had begun to find its way through cracks in the cave roof, forming little waterfalls. "Tom, look!" Hellen pointed back over Tom's shoulder at the water streaming from the roof, but he just kept rowing and did not turn around. Hellen was worried about him. She had never seen him so grim and determined.

In a few minutes, they had reached the huge tower and now drifted beside it. From the shore, it had looked like the steeple atop a small village church. *How deceptive distance can be*, Hellen thought. The circular tower was enormous. It loomed from the water like the tip of an iceberg, tilted slightly, its golden, onion-shaped dome almost reaching the roof of the cave.

"Impossible," Hellen said, looking up at her distorted reflection in the golden bulb. "The oldest known dome in this style is part of the Cathedral of the Dormition in Moscow—it wasn't built until 1475, 250 years after Kitezh was founded," Hellen said, unable to contain her amazement.

"Fascinating," Tom replied, his face a stony mask. He got to his feet and, reaching up, was able to grab hold of the edge of the small window below the golden dome. Without a word, he pulled himself up and crawled through the window, then turned and reached back down to help Hellen.

"No tricks, or my good friend Qadir might be forced to harm your dear Cloutard."

Hellen stood to grasp Tom's hand and he pulled her up after him. Inside, the tower was about fifteen feet in diameter. Their flashlight beams shone into fathomless darkness. A narrow staircase spiraled downward around the inside wall of the tower. There was no railing, and Tom and Hellen stuck close to the wall as they made their way down.

"Do you have any idea how to get us out of this?" Hellen asked.

Tom ignored her question, shining his flashlight on the walls of the tower. "Why isn't the tower filled with water?" he wondered aloud. "It's what they call a hydrostatic paradox, isn't it? The water inside should be just as high as the water outside."

Hellen often forgot that Tom was actually an unusually intelligent guy. Normally, all he let people see was the overgrown kid.

"I don't know why . . ." Hellen admitted. "But let's count ourselves lucky we don't have to dive again," she added as they continued downward.

They had to hop over an occasional gap in the stairs, and as they approached the bottom they could see that the floor of the tower was submerged. "There's your water," Hellen said.

At the foot of the tower the water was hip-deep and trickling in from the lake through cracks in the walls created by the last foreshock. Slowly but inexorably, the tower was filling with icy water.

"What now?" Tom said.

Hellen shrugged and shone her flashlight around. "Here's the answer to your hydro question. There are no doors or windows down here. It's a completely closed system. Presumably, someone sealed the tower from the outside a long time ago. Maybe to make it harder to access?" Hellen speculated, as she stepped into the bitterly cold water.

"Well, it looks like the systems are starting to reconnect," said Tom. "We'd better hurry."

Hellen waded in a circle, shining her light on the tower floor. "There's something down here. Give me another flare."

"They're up top in your rucksack, but I've still got a few of these." He withdrew three six-inch-long glow sticks from a side pocket of his overalls. As he stepped into the water himself, he bent the sticks and a blue glow slowly filled the room.

"Blue light," Hellen said. "For some reason, it makes me think of Rambo." She grinned at Tom, and a smile also flashed on his face, if only for a second. Tom threw the sticks into different places in the water and he and

Hellen stepped back and looked at the huge relief that shimmered in the blue light of the glow sticks.

"This has no business being here," Hellen said in surprise. "We're in deepest Russia and as far as I can tell, this is a Nordic rune circle. These characters were used as far back as the Vikings."

"The Vikings? Can you read it?"

"Lucky for us, I happen to know Norse code," Hellen said.

They looked at each other and both burst out laughing. For a few seconds, they were able to forget that they were sitting in a cave that might collapse at any time, that Tom's grandfather and Father Lazarev were dead, and that Cloutard was being held hostage. For a few seconds, everything was good between them again.

"And you call me an overgrown kid?" Tom said, giving her an affectionate nudge.

Hellen's eyes grew melancholy. "We were good together, you and I. What happened to us? Why exactly aren't we together anymore?"

The moment was rudely interrupted by another ominous rumbling, bringing both of them back to the urgency of their situation.

"Okay," Tom said. "If these are Nordic runes, and we're looking for artifacts from Nordic mythology, then we're in the right place. But I don't see anything like the chest that Father Lazarev mentioned."

"I think I've got an idea," Hellen said, and a second later she ducked underwater. She picked up one of the glow sticks and examined the rune circle more closely. Tom could see that it was actually a series of concentric circles, and Hellen was now running her hand over some of the runes.

"I think I've got it. It's a kind of Caesar cipher," she said when she resurfaced. "Let me think for a minute."

"As far as I'm concerned you can take as long as you like, but I'm not sure if Mother Nature is going to wait for you," Tom replied.

She said nothing, but simply stood and stared at the runes. Then she dived down again. She pushed the concentric circles as if turning the dials of a combination lock, and they moved with surprising ease. Tom heard a grinding, scraping noise, muffled by the water, as she turned each of the circles, sometimes in one direction, sometimes in the other. In between, she came back to the surface to breathe.

"One more and I've got it," she said, after diving several times.

Suddenly, gas bubbles rose to the surface as the center circle jolted upward with a grating noise. A small pillar rose about eighteen inches from the flooded floor. Tom's eyes widened as he saw a compartment built into the stone column. Inside it was a tall, narrow box—it had to be the chest that Father Lazarev had spoken of.

"Don't just stand there like a statue. Help me!" Hellen said. Carefully, they lifted the long chest out of its compartment. Then they retreated a short way up the spiral stairs to get out of the icy water and set the chest on a step. They'd found it! They looked at each other with a mixture of joy and relief.

Without warning, the earth trembled again, the low rumble bringing them back to the moment. Without a word, they picked up the chest and began their ascent, Hellen leading the way. Stones fell past them into the depths. More cracks appeared, and water began shooting in through more and more fractures in the wall.

"Can't we just wait for the tower to fill up and then swim? That sounds easier to me," Hellen panted.

"Sure, but what if the tower caves in? No, we have to get out of here as fast as we can."

The earth shuddered again, and Tom looked up just in time. "Watch out!" he shouted. Hellen let go of the chest and jumped forward just as one of the tower bells fell directly between them. With a loud gong, it took a huge chunk out of the stairway and tumbled on into the depths. Tom was just able to hold onto the chest and press himself back against the wall.

"Are you all right?" they heard Brice call down from above. "I don't want you kicking the bucket down there."

"Your concern is truly heartwarming," Tom shouted back. Two more circles around the tower and they would be back at the window.

A fracture appeared where the bell had destroyed the stairs, and a jet of water shot from the wall. The water was pushing away tiles on the inside of the tower, making the hole bigger by the second.

"Take the chest," Tom ordered, holding it out to Hellen.

"What about you?"

"Don't worry about me. Take it!" Hellen looked fearfully into Tom's eyes. "*Take it!*" he yelled at her. Stunned, she did as he said and reached for the chest. Balancing precariously, Tom lifted the chest over the top of the jet of water that separated them. Hellen grabbed hold of it and pulled it over to her.

"Go. I'll be right behind you." Hellen hesitated a moment longer, then turned and hurried up the stairs, even as the wall continued to crack and the water tore at the stairway.

She reached the window where they had entered the tower. The Welshman was standing in the wobbly boat, waiting impatiently for Tom and Hellen to return. "Did you find it?" Hellen nodded and handed the chest down to him through the window. "Where's Wagner?"

"He's right behind me," she said as she climbed onto the edge of the window. She turned around just as another shock thundered through the cave, making the tower shudder, and she slipped from the window and fell awkwardly into the boat. A boulder cracked free from the roof of the cave and fell directly onto the dome.

"*Tom!*" Hellen screamed as the tower collapsed and sank into the blackness of the lake.

67

BENEATH THE CHURCH OF OUR LADY OF KAZAN, LAKE SVETLOYAR

"Where is Tom?!" Cloutard asked as he helped pull the boat ashore. Hellen shook her head absently and stared at nothing. Her eyes said it all.

"Wagner's doing a little sightseeing," the Welshman said with a laugh. He waved Qadir over and handed him the chest.

Hellen climbed out of the boat and Cloutard took her in his arms. Now she could let it out, and she burst into tears. Cloutard held her tightly and pressed his cheek against her head. It felt like an eternity before Hellen slowly began to collect herself again. She did not want to leave Cloutard's protective embrace, but Qadir came and separated them.

"That's enough weeping and wailing," the Welshman said. "It's Ms. de May, isn't it? I really am terribly sorry about what happened to your friend . . ." He paused for a moment, then went on with amusement, "Actually, I'm not sorry at all. I'm glad I'm finally rid of the troublemaker." He laughed spitefully and stared at Hellen. She would have tried to throttle him if Cloutard hadn't held her back, and the soldiers raised their Kalashnikovs to keep her in check.

"You despicable asshole," Hellen hissed. "I promise you'll pay for what happened to him."

Brice and Qadir laughed out loud.

"And just how to you plan to do that, little lady? It's quite possible that you'll join your friend out there—we haven't decided that yet," Brice said, pointing out over the lake. "Now, whether that happens depends entirely on how well you continue to cooperate. So far, you've been extremely sensible." He went over to the chest and crouched over it. There was no visible lock, just the two handles, one on each end. "Now, how do I get this thing open?" Annoyed, he grasped it by the handles and shook it roughly.

"I don't know," Hellen said. "I only had the thing in my hands a few minutes, and I had other things to deal with than figuring out how to open it. I don't know any more than you do."

The Welshman stood up again and went back to Hellen and Cloutard.

"Well, now, that's exactly what I don't believe." He took out his .22 revolver and shot Cloutard in the thigh. François cried out and fell to the ground, cursing. Blood pulsed from the wound.

"*Fils de pute*," Cloutard muttered, pressing one hand onto the wound.

"You insane fucking bastard!" Hellen screamed at Brice.

"Do you kiss your mother with that mouth? Let's try again, shall we? How do I get this damned box open?" The Welshman moved uncomfortably close to Hellen and stared into her eyes threateningly. She turned her face away.

"You obviously haven't studied the legends of Kitezh deeply enough," Hellen said. "Otherwise you'd know that *only the pure of heart can see the truth*. And as you've so impressively shown, you are anything but." She knelt beside Cloutard, took off her belt and wrapped it around his leg. Slowly, to avoid the impression that he was reaching for a weapon, Cloutard reached into his jacket pocket for his hip flask and drank a mouthful of the 3000-dollar-a-bottle cognac. Then he looked sadly from the flask to his wound, took a final swig, and poured the rest of the liquid over the wound. He grimaced in pain as Hellen, with the belt and a piece of fabric from her overalls, applied a makeshift pressure bandage to stem the flow of blood.

In a rage, the Welshman stomped to one of his soldiers, grabbed his Kalashnikov, racked the bolt, and pointed the gun at Hellen and Cloutard, who were cowering on the ground.

"That's exactly what I mean," Hellen said. "Go ahead, shoot. We're not going to help you anymore." Cloutard looked at Hellen with admiration, then nodded in agreement.

"Aaarrrgghh!" Brice screamed, and he turned and emptied the entire magazine at the chest in one sustained burst. Everyone ducked for cover, and even Qadir flinched. Sparks flew and ricochets whistled past their heads, but miraculously no one was hit. When the smoke cleared, all eyes locked onto the chest, but it had not suffered a single scratch.

"That's impo—"

But that was as far as the Welshman got. And for Hellen, the next few moments passed in slow motion. At first, she did not hear the rumbling or feel the swaying, but she saw chunks of rock, large and small, falling from the roof and slamming into the cave floor like grenades. And despite the utter hopelessness of their situation, she somehow knew with crystal clarity: *I will not die today.*

Just then, a boulder fell directly onto one of the soldiers, crushing him. The other two soldiers were knocked over, then scrambled to their feet and ran for the passage that led back out. Brice and Qadir were also thrown off balance.

"Where are you going, you cowards?" Brice bellowed after the soldiers. "Help me!"

"Sorry. No amount of money is worth dying for here," one of them shouted back. The soldiers disappeared along the path by which they'd entered, and for a moment everything fell quiet. But not for long.

Qadir was just straightening up again when, as if from nowhere, Tom appeared on the shore and threw himself at Brice's henchman.

"Tom?" Hellen stared open-mouthed as he battled Qadir on the cave floor in front of her. For a moment, Tom gained the upper hand, landing a hard, angry blow on Qadir's nose. In the meantime, Brice had regained his feet and was reaching out for the chest. But just then another shock rocked the cave, this one more powerful than any before it. His fingers missed the handle of the chest and it slid away in Hellen's direction. She grabbed one of the handles just in time to stop it from sliding into the lake.

Qadir had managed to break free of Tom and was standing when the next lull came. "Is that all you've got?" he said. He grasped his broken nose in one hand and wrenched it straight with a sickening crack. Even Tom flinched at the sound, and Qadir waved him forward.

"Come on, finish him off," Brice egged Qadir on. Like boxers, the two men circled each other.

"I hope you washed your hands this time. Something like that could easily get infected," said Tom, pointing at Qadir's nose. If Qadir hadn't already known that it was Tom who'd dragged him into the lavatory in Yurino, he knew now. Suddenly, the earth lurched and groaned again, and everyone grabbed the nearest boulder and held on. Part of the cave floor buckled and a deep chasm opened up behind Qadir, who struggled to keep his balance. Tom darted forward and booted him in the chest, and Qadir stumbled back and fell with a final scream into the gaping abyss.

When the tremor finally settled, Hellen looked around. Brice had vanished. She jumped to her feet and threw her arms around Tom.

"Are we already dead, or are you here to lead us to the afterlife?" asked Cloutard, still lying on the cave floor and not entirely convinced that Tom was actually standing in front of him.

They had made it through another tremor, but surviving the next was looking more and more unlikely. They had to escape the cave as quickly as they could, but their only exit had been cut off by the enormous rift that had swallowed Qadir.

"How are we going to get out now?" Cloutard said.

But Tom and Hellen were not listening. They were gazing into each other's eyes. Hellen still could not believe he'd made it. She pinched his upper arm.

"Ow!"

"Just checking," she said. Then she leaned forward slowly, beckoning to Tom to kiss her.

Cloutard rolled his eyes and lifted his hip flask to take another drink, only to realize in horror that he'd already emptied it.

"*Merde!*" he swore as he looked up at his friends.

Tom accepted Hellen's invitation, pulling her close and leaning down. But just as they were about to kiss, they were interrupted by a familiar voice.

"So really: why *exactly* aren't you two still together?" asked Arthur Julius Prey, wearing a broad grin.

68

BENEATH THE CHURCH OF OUR LADY OF KAZAN

Silence fell for a moment as they processed what they were seeing. Tom and Hellen cried "Grandpop!" simultaneously, and then glanced sheepishly at one another.

"It's not a dinosaur, but it should get us out of here," Arthur said, and he clapped the palm of his hand on the rusty steel plate of the vessel that had just surfaced in the subterranean lake.

Tom's grandfather was looking at them from the open hatch of an aging civilian research submersible. The observation dome in the bow was two-thirds submerged, but they could see Father Lazarev inside, waving enthusiastically.

"*Fantastique!*" Cloutard shouted, and he tried to stand up.

"You coming? Or were you planning to wait for the next tremor?" Arthur waved them aboard and disappeared inside the sub.

"A little help?" Cloutard said. Tom and Hellen hurried to him and heaved him onto his feet. Together, they helped him negotiate the narrow hatch, and Hellen climbed down after him.

Then the real quake struck, shattering the silence. The foreshocks had been bad enough, but they were nothing compared to this. A boulder the size of a car fell from the cave roof, missing the submersible by a hair's breadth and sending a wall of water over the vessel, almost capsizing it.

"The chest!" Hellen screamed as loud as she could to make herself heard over the earthquake. She had reappeared at the hatch just in time to get soaked by the wave. Tom nodded and ran back, struggling to keep his footing. The chest began to slip, but he leaped after it just in time to stop it from sliding into the newly-opened chasm. He wrapped his arms around it and zigzagged back to the submersible, dodging falling rocks. He jumped onto the deck and passed the chest down through the hatch. Then he looked up and froze—where the tower had been, the cave ceiling was collapsing with a roar. Brilliant sunlight shone through the gap; the rays filtering through the dust looked almost divine.

"Tom! What are you waiting for?" Hellen called from the hatch. But for a few heartbeats, he simply stood and stared in wonder at the spectacle. Then a chunk of rock the size of a tennis ball clanged against the steel submersible, jolting him out of his reverie, and he slipped through the hatch. They had to hurry: in a few moments, the entire cave would collapse and bury them beneath it.

Arthur locked the hatch. Small stones fell like hail on the outer skin of the submersible as the five of them squeezed together in the tiny, rusting cabin.

"All aboard?" Father Lazarev asked, then said, "Then let's go!" And the vessel dove in a flurry of bubbles.

Father Lazarev smiled knowingly as he switched on the submersible's floodlights, and everyone held their breath. The sight in front of them was something they would not forget as long as they lived. Huddled close together, they gazed through the observation dome. The floodlights illuminated the ruins of Kitezh on the lake floor, which only hinted at the city's former magnificence. Like meteorites striking the earth in slow motion, countless rocks and boulders sank onto the city, destroying the last semi-intact structures. Despite the spectacular nature of the event, a somber mood filled the sub.

Without warning, a boulder struck them, shaking the vessel and its occupants.

"Head for the light, over there," said Tom, pointing toward the place where the church tower had loomed from the water, and Father Lazarev steered the submersible in the direction Tom pointed, skillfully dodging sinking rocks.

"Watch out!" Hellen cried, throwing her hands over her face. The sub tipped to the right, then back to the left. Again and again, stones crashed against the hull.

"The possibility of successfully navigating an asteroid field is approximately 3,720 to 1," Cloutard said.

"Nice one," said Tom, and he and Arthur nodded appreciatively.

"Could you *please* save the film quotes until we're not all about to die?" Hellen said, and everyone laughed, if only briefly.

"Hold on!" Father Lazarev cried as he sent the sub suddenly into a vertical dive. A section of the roof the size of a football field had broken free and was plunging toward the bottom of the lake. A rock that size would crush them like an insect, but at the last second the submersible scraped past the enormous piece of the roof. Once they were safely on the other side, brilliant sunlight flooded the tiny cabin. The occupants of the submersible raised their hands protectively to shield themselves from the light. Like a rubber duck, the vessel popped to the surface and floated, bobbing on the lake.

Everyone cheered and hugged—the earthquake was over, and they had made it. They were alive. Tom opened the hatch and looked out. It was a beautiful day, the sun high in a cloudless sky.

He looked around in amazement. A new and much larger lake had been created by the earthquake and the collapse of the cave. He smiled when he saw the Church of Our Lady of Kazan, which seemed to have made it through the quake in one piece. Tom pointed Father Lazarev in the right direction, and they motored toward the church. At the shore, they all climbed out.

"I have to ask: where the hell did you get a submarine?" Tom said as they climbed the embankment that led to the church.

"It's like I told you: I made it my life's mission to explore Kitezh. And this seemed like the right vessel for the job."

"I asked him the same question," said Arthur. "And I didn't get a clear answer either." He paused, then went on casually, "If you ask me, he got it from one of his KGB buddies."

"The KGB?" Hellen, Cloutard and Tom asked as one.

"I could tell you, but then I'd have to kill you," the old priest said with an impish smile. "But I can tell you this much: after the USSR disintegrated, you could get almost anything on the black market . . ."

Tom and Cloutard nodded. They'd heard this before.

". . . including this prototype submersible. I had—"

But Father Lazarev did not get to finish his sentence. Without warning, an enormous explosion destroyed the jeep, which had been parked in front of the church. The blast knocked all of them off their feet.

69

SUITE AT THE HOTEL ASTORIA, LENINGRAD, 1987

Berlin Brice opened his eyes just as the woman emerged from the bathroom. He was an atheist, but at the sight of her he could almost believe there really was a God. A body so flawless, so stunningly beautiful, uniting style and charisma in one perfect being—that could only be the handiwork of the Almighty.

They had been living in the suite for almost three months, enjoying the life that Leningrad offered. Brice's shady business ventures had provided him with excellent contacts in the Communist Party. As a result, they enjoyed countless privileges and could live in luxury.

"Why do you look at me that way, *solnishka*?" she asked, slipping back into bed.

"Because you're perfect. And because I have never been happier than I am with you. You know me. I'm not one for sentimentality, and love has always been a foreign word for me. But with you . . ."

They kissed passionately. And though they had made love not even half an hour before, their desire instantly flared again.

Such a pity this woman is married, Brice thought. *A real waste, especially when I think who she's married to.*

But their embraces drove all thought from his mind. She rolled him onto his back and positioned herself on top of him. Every time he entered her he found himself wishing it could be forever. If there were a perfect way to die, it would be in the arms of this woman.

She leaned down to him and whispered in his ear. "I have bad news. I have to leave tomorrow." Her words hit Brice like a bolt of lightning. "My husband is coming home from his travels . . ." She faltered, and Brice saw immediately that she was struggling inside.

"What is it? What's the matter?" he asked, and he stroked her cheek.

"I have to sleep with my husband as soon as I can," she said, regret filling her words.

"Why in the world would you have to do that?"

"To make him believe that the child in my belly is his."

Suddenly, fury welled up inside Brice. If she was truly going back to the priest, then she would come to regret it. Berlin Brice would not be rejected.

70

PRESENT DAY, IN FRONT OF THE CHURCH OF OUR LADY
OF KAZAN, LAKE SVETLOYAR

Tom was the first to recover from the shock, only to look up into the barrel of a Kalashnikov, behind it the eyes of Father Fjodor. It took Tom a few moments to realize what he was seeing. As Hellen had suspected, Father Fjodor's injury had been no more than superficial—he was very much alive now.

"I hope I have your full attention now," Father Fjodor said.

When Father Lazarev realized what had happened, he gazed at his son with sad eyes. "Does it still surprise you that I did not pass the legacy of the guardians of Kitezh on to you?" he asked. His words were full of reproach and regret.

"Give me the chest with the Nibelung treasure," Fjodor snapped at his father. "It would have made no difference what I did—it was never good enough for you anyway." Father Lazarev said nothing. "The guardianship must be passed from father to son. You robbed me of my rightful inheritance." Father Fjodor's voice was filled with hatred.

"I hate to butt in, but the way you're carrying on, all I can say to Father Lazarev is: congratulations, good decision," Tom said.

"*Se taire*," said Cloutard placatingly to Tom. He, too, had just recovered from the shock of the blast, but with his injured leg he stayed on the ground. The others were all back on their feet.

Arthur laid a hand on Tom's shoulder. "Tom, he's got a gun," he said. Tom turned to his grandfather, and the old man could see it in Tom's face: I know, and I don't give a damn. "I just wanted to make sure," Arthur said.

Father Fjodor moved to Tom and pressed the barrel of the Kalashnikov against his forehead.

"Stay out of it. This is between father and son," Fjodor snarled through bared teeth. "Bring me the chest," he said, his voice again under control.

Tom, his hands raised, went to where the chest lay. It had fallen off to one side after the explosion. He picked it up and dropped it at Father Fjodor's feet, then took a step back.

"How do you open this thing?" Fjodor said, turning back to his father.

"Only the pure of heart—"

"Shut up with that pure-of-heart shit!" Fjodor shouted.

"All you are doing is continuing to prove how unworthy of the guardianship you are."

"Unworthy? Me? Why shouldn't I be worthy?"

"You have no idea how difficult the decision was for me. For years, I tried to see righteousness in you. For years, I tried to make you understand the duty that would fall to you, and how important it would be to use the power responsibly. To my disgrace, I failed. I never understood why you turned to the cloth and took your vows. The priesthood does not suit your nature."

"What do you know about it, old man? You always made me feel that I wasn't good enough, not for you or for the world. But religion isn't just about faith. It's about politics, too. Do you think I could have made it as far as I have with good deeds and piousness?"

Father Lazarev sighed with disappointment. Tom looked into his face and saw the anguish he was suffering.

"And unlike you," Fjodor went on, snarling at the old man, "I've never been responsible for another person's death."

Father Lazarev looked at him in confusion.

"Did you think I didn't know?" Fjodor bellowed. "I know everything!"

"What do you know? I don't have any idea what you're talking about," Father Lazarev said, perplexed. He looked at the others around him, as if one of them might be able to help.

"You killed my mother. You murdered your own wife."

"I . . . what?"

"You sent a KGB killer to poison her."

Father Lazarev shook his head. He tried to say something, but his son spoke first: "Don't try to deny it. I know the truth, all of it. You found out Mother was having an affair and that I was not your son. So you took revenge on her and handed the dirty work to a KGB assassin."

The old priest's face turned white. He struggled for words and air. He seemed not only stunned, but also completely unable to understand what Fjodor had just thrown at him.

"What do you mean, you're not my son? What do you mean, your mother had an affair?" His words came in short bursts, he was having trouble breathing, and he suddenly looked years older.

"Don't act like you haven't known about it for years. My true father told me everything. He sent me the letters Mother wrote to him, and he showed me proof that your KGB contacts were responsible for her death."

"Then . . . then who is your true father?" The old man's voice was a resigned whisper.

"Berlin Brice!"

"Wow," Tom whispered to Cloutard. "Father Lazarev can be happy this guy's not his son. He's not only a psychopath, he's also exceptionally stupid."

"You're a self-righteous old man. And a damned murderer," Fjodor spat.

Father Lazarev had given up the fight. These revelations were too much for him, and he closed his eyes. A tear trickled down his cheek.

"And now I'd finally like to find out how to open this damned chest."

A crash made Fjodor spin around. The church door had banged shut, out of the blue. Fjodor turned back to the others.

"Where's your friend? Where is Hellen?"

71

CHURCH OF OUR LADY OF KAZAN

Everyone looked around, but Hellen was nowhere in sight.

"Do you know where she is?" Cloutard whispered to Tom.

"Nope," Tom replied. "But I hope she's not doing anything silly."

Father Fjodor looked around in confusion. He pointed the barrel of the rifle toward the church.

"All of you come with me!"

The small group headed for the church. Tom, arriving first, went to open the door.

"Nice and slow," said Father Fjodor. Tom opened the door and went in first, then Father Fjodor hustled his father and Arthur, with Cloutard supported between them, inside. They looked around. The church was empty. Cloutard and Tom looked at each other, puzzled.

"Miss de Mey," Father Fjodor called. "Come out, come out, wherever you are. You have no chance. Your friends will die if you don't show yourself."

In one corner of the church, a tall candle holder crashed to the floor. Fjodor spun around and fired into the corner, but there was nothing to see. Father Lazarev smiled slyly.

"Miss de Mey, I'm warning you," Fjodor said. "I'm prepared to go to any length. I haven't been searching for the Nibelung treasure for so long to give up now. If you don't come out—"

Another sound, this time from near the entrance. Father Fjodor whirled around and fired several shots. He was growing more and more nervous. Cloutard had stretched out on a pew, resting his leg. Arthur and Tom exchanged a surprised look. Slowly, they moved apart, putting the priest between them. Suddenly, a window over the small altar shattered. Tom and Arthur immediately seized the opportunity. Cloutard had already realized what they were planning to do, and he tossed his cap across the church, past Fjodor on the right. Fjodor saw the motion from the corner of his eye and spun around, by now so confused that Tom's job was easy. He threw himself on the surprised priest from behind and in less than a second had disarmed him and pinned him to the floor. Injured and fighting a trained soldier, Father Fjodor had no chance at all. Tom handed the AK-47 to Arthur, who immediately pointed it at Fjodor. Just then, Hellen ran in through the front door.

"Did I miss anything?"

"Where have you been?" Tom asked.

"I was knocked out. What happened? I didn't see anything."

She was grinning broadly, and Tom knew that she was lying through her teeth.

"Only the pure of heart . . ." Father Lazarev murmured as they left the church.

"You used the cloak of invisibility and now you are denying it," Cloutard chided Hellen.

"I have no idea what you're talking about," Hellen said, giving him a wink.

"And my damned Louis XIII is empty. Where am I going to find a decent bottle of cognac in the Russian boondocks?" Cloutard said with a sigh.

"Maybe the cavalry can help you with that," said Tom, and he pointed at the convoy of Russian military vehicles just turning off the main road and heading in their direction.

"Mother will bail us out," said Hellen, smiling at Tom.

"She has to be good for something," said Tom. Then he pulled Hellen close and kissed her on the forehead.

72

BANQUET HALL AT THE KREMLIN, NIZHNY NOVGOROD

"I think I would've preferred the Russky-Cossacksocks opera," Tom sighed.

"The composer's name is Rimsky-Korsakov, you heathen," said Hellen.

The Russian president had been delivering a speech in his native language for the last thirty minutes. Finally, however, he handed the microphone over to Theresia de Mey, who stepped up to the podium amid a round of applause. She was there on behalf of UNESCO, and to hand over the cross of Kitezh to the Russian state.

"Let's hope your mom sticks to the old rule about speeches at parties," Tom whispered.

"You can talk about anything, as long as you keep it under five minutes," Tom's grandfather said from the row behind.

"Right on the money, Grandpop," Tom said.

And, in fact, Theresia merely handed the cross to the governor of Nizhny Novgorod, said a few words of thanks to the team, shook a few hands, and exited the stage again.

"I had no idea anyone in your family could keep it short," Tom said to Hellen, and smiled. Hellen's reproachful eye roll was obligatory, as was Cloutard's grin.

"Time for shots!" the Frenchman said, stopping a passing waiter and relieving him of an entire tray of chilled vodka shots. Cloutard immediately downed two of the small glasses and distributed the rest among Tom, Hellen, Arthur, Father Lazarev, and Theresia de Mey.

"*Tvoye zdorovie*," Cloutard cried as they clinked glasses. They knocked back the vodka together, and then as one made the same face: *Oooahhh.* Without warning, Cloutard smashed his empty glass on the floor with all his strength.

A deathly silence settled over the hall. Every one of the hundred or so invited guests turned and stared at Cloutard.

"*Merde*," he murmured, looking around sheepishly. "I thought that was still a custom here."

"*Tvoye zdorovie!*" the Russian president called, breaking the painful silence. He emptied his glass in a single draft and, like Cloutard, smashed it on the floor.

"*Tvoye zdorovie!*" the other guests shouted as one, raising their glasses—and then all hell broke loose as a hundred glasses shattered on the floor. Cloutard let out a sigh of relief.

"Thank you for bringing something for Blue Shield this time, a wonderful artifact that we can loan to the museums," said Theresia proudly, embracing her daughter.

"The Sword of Siegfried," Hellen murmured, shaking her head: she still could not believe it. Until just recently, she had considered the Nibelung story to be no more than what it always had been: a legend. Now she knew that the cloak of invisibility and Siegfried's sword actually existed. What else was out there? What else would they discover in the name of Blue Shield? Hellen looked dreamily around the room, sipping slowly at the second shot Cloutard had handed her just moments earlier.

Arthur seemed to have read Hellen's thoughts and came over to her. "It is truly impressive just how many wonders the world has in store for us. I do believe that you are at the very beginning of a journey to rediscover the great secrets of the past. A pity, really, that I can't keep helping you with it." Tom's grandfather's eyes were aglow with enthusiasm.

No wonder Tom's such an adventure fanatic—even his grandfather can't get enough of it, Hellen thought.

"I agree. I also hate being stuck behind a desk," said Vittoria Arcano, Theresia's right-hand woman, who had just picked her way across broken shards of glass and through a throng of guests to join them. Cloutard immediately handed her a shot.

"Well, now that we have this little side trip behind us," said Theresia, smiling around the group, "do you think you might finally turn your attention to your actual assignment?"

Vittoria handed each of them a dossier—the files that the three of them already knew only too well.

Cloutard's face lit up as he took his copy. "Ah yes, the search for—"

"Sshhh, not here!" said Tom, glancing furtively into the file containing their next adventure. "We already know the walls in Russia have ears."

73

SOMEWHERE IN NEW MEXICO

The officer at the gate watched the approaching Mercedes GLE Coupe curiously at it drew closer. As a rule, non-military personnel never visited the secret maximum-security facility. If he hadn't been informed about the visit a few minutes earlier, he would already have sounded the alarm. But his instructions came from the very top, and he had asked no questions. "A high-ranking FBI agent will be arriving to interrogate a prisoner," his superior officer had told him.

"Papers please, sir," he said when the car pulled up. The man handed him a letter and his FBI identification, but said nothing. The officer checked the man's papers and ran everything through the usual security checks. Nothing unusual. His computer gave him the green light to let the man enter the high-security wing.

"Thank you, sir. Welcome to the site. Major Tanner is expecting you and will show you to the interview room, as requested."

The man nodded and parked his car in the space allotted to him. Once he had passed through a series of additional security measures, he was led into an interview room. Apart from a table and two chairs, the room was bare. No windows, no one-way mirror.

"The microphones and cameras have been deactivated, sir, as stipulated in the instructions we received from FBI headquarters. The detainee will be along shortly."

The man nodded and Major Tanner left the room. Seconds later, the door opened again and a slim, dark-skinned woman, her hands and feet shackled, was led in.

Ossana Ibori looked at the man. When he stood and walked over to her, she looked him up and down, raising her eyebrows in amazement.

"So it worked," she said.

A triumphant grin appeared momentarily on Noah's face. Until just recently, he had been unable to leave his wheelchair—a fate for which he had Tom Wagner to thank.

"Your assassin failed. Wagner's still alive. And to add insult to injury, Tom killed his brother, so your assassin is . . . upset."

Ossana was about to say something, but Noah raised his hand angrily.

"And they've recovered the Nibelung treasure! Why didn't we know about that?"

"Because not even Palffy was all-knowing," Ossana said defensively. "There was nothing about it in his papers."

Noah smiled disarmingly. His status within the organization had undoubtedly improved if even Ossana was explaining herself to him. And now that the organization—in fact, the man at the very top—had enabled him to walk again, they could be sure of his unconditional loyalty.

"It doesn't matter. It was not easy to find out where you were. The Americans take their 'persons of interest' very seriously. But we have extended our range of influence, as you can see."

"When am I getting out of this shithole?" Ossana asked.

"Soon. We still need to make a few arrangements."

"Does Daddy have a new project yet?"

"Yes. And this time we know how to stop Wagner and his little crew from getting in our way."

"A trap?"

"Better. Much better."

—THE END—
OF THE INVISIBLE CITY

Tom Wagner and his team will return in
THE GOLDEN PATH

THE TOM WAGNER SERIES

THE STONE OF DESTINY

(Tom Wagner Prequel)

A dark secret of the Habsburg Empire. A treasure believed to be lost long time ago. A breathless hunt into the past.

The thriller "The Stone of Destiny" leads Tom Wagner and Hellen de Mey into the dark past of the Habsburgs and to a treasure that seems to have been lost for a long time.

The breathless hunt goes through half of Europe and the surprise at the end is not missing: A conspiracy that began in the last days of the First World War reaches up to the present day!

**Free Download!
Click here or open link:**
https://robertsmaclay.com/start-free

THE SACRED WEAPON

(A Tom Wagner Adventure 1)

A demonic plan. A mysterious power. An extraordinary team.

The Notre Dame fire, the theft of the Shroud of Turin and a terrorist attack on the legendary Meteora monasteries are just the beginning. Fear has gripped Europe.

Stolen relics, a mysterious power with a demonic plan and allies with questionable allegiances: Tom Wagner is in a race against time, trying to prevent a disaster that could tear Europe down to its foundations. And there's no one he can trust...

Click here or open link:
https://robertsmaclay.com/1-tw

THE LIBRARY OF THE KINGS

(A Tom Wagner Adventure 2)

Hidden wisdom. A relic of unbelievable power. A race against time.

Ancient legends, devilish plans, startling plot twists, breathtaking action and a dash of humor: *Library of the Kings* is gripping entertainment – a Hollywood blockbuster in book form.

When clues to the long-lost Library of Alexandria surface, ex-Cobra officer Tom Wagner and archaeologist Hellen de Mey aren't the only ones on the hunt for its vanished secrets. A sinister power is plotting in the background, and nothing is as it seems. And the dark secret hidden in the Library threatens all of humanity.

Click here or open link:
https://robertsmaclay.com/2-tw

―――

THE INVISIBLE CITY

(A Tom Wagner Adventure 3)

A vanished civilization. A diabolical trap. A mystical treasure.

Tom Wagner, archaeologist Hellen de Mey and gentleman crook Francois Cloutard are about to embark on their first official assignment from Blue Shield – but when Tom receives an urgent call from the Vatican, things start to move quickly:

With the help of the Patriarch of the Russian Orthodox Church, they discover clues to an age-old myth: the Russian Atlantis. And a murderous race to find an ancient, long-lost relic leads them from Cuba to the Russian hinterlands.

What mystical treasure lies buried beneath Nizhny Novgorod? Who laid the evil trap? And what does it all have to do with Tom's grandfather?

Click here or open link:

https://robertsmaclay.com/3-tw

―――

THE GOLDEN PATH

(A Tom Wagner Adventure 4)

The greatest treasure of mankind. An international intrigue. A cruel revelation.

Now a special unit for Blue Shield, Tom and his team are on a search for the legendary El Dorado. But, as usual, things don't go as planned.

The team gets separated and is – literally – forced to fight a battle on multiple fronts: Hellen and Cloutard make discoveries that overturn the familiar story of El Dorado's gold.

Meanwhile, the President of the United States has tasked Tom with keeping a dangerous substance out of the hands of terrorists.

Click here or open link:
https://robertsmaclay.com/4-tw

―――

THE ROUND TABLE CHRONICLE

(A Tom Wagner Adventure 5)

The first secret society of mankind. Artifacts of inestimable power. A race you cannot win.

The events turn upside down: Tom Wagner is missing. Hellen's father has turned up and a hot lead is waiting for the Blue Shield team: The legendary Chronicle of the Round Table.

What does the Chronicles of the Round Table of King Arthur say? Must the history around Avalon and Camelot be rewritten? Where is Tom and who is pulling the strings?

Coming Fall 2021

THRILLED READER REVIEWS

"Suspense and entertainment! I've read a lot of books like this one; some better, some worse. This is one of the best books in this genre I've ever read. I'm really looking forward to a good sequel. "

———

"I just couldn't put this book down. Full of surprising plot twists, humor, and action! "

———

"An explosive combination of Robert Langdon, James Bond & Indiana Jones"

———

"Good build-up of tension; I was always wondering what happens next. Toward the end, where the story gets more and more complex and constantly changes scenes, I was on the edge of my seat"

———

"Great! I read all three books in one sitting. Dan Brown better watch his back."

———

"The best thing about it is the basic premise, a story with historical background knowledge scattered throughout the book–never too much at one time and always supporting the plot"

―――――

"Entertaining and action-packed! The carefully thought-out story has a clear plotline, but there are a couple of unexpected twists as well. I really enjoyed it. The sections of the book are tailored to maximize the suspense, they don't waste any time with unimportant details. The chapters are short and compact–perfect for a half-hour commute or at night before turning out the lights. Recommended to all lovers of the genre and anyone interested in getting to know it better. I'll definitely read the sequel."

―――――

"Anyone who likes reading Dan Brown, James Rollins and Preston & Child needs to get this book."

―――――

"An exciting build-up, interesting and historically significant settings, surprising plot twists in the right places."

ABOUT THE AUTHORS
ROBERTS & MACLAY

Roberts & Maclay have known each other for over 25 years, are good friends and have worked together on various projects.

The fact that they are now also writing thrillers together is less coincidence than fate. Talking shop about films, TV series and suspense novels has always been one of their favorite pastimes.

———

M.C. Roberts is the pen name of an successful entrepreneur and blogger. Adventure stories have always been his passion: after recording a number of superhero audiobooks on his father's old tape recorder as a six-year-old, he postponed his dream of writing novels for almost 40 years, and worked as a marketing director, editor-in-chief, DJ, opera critic, communication coach, blogger, online marketer and author of trade books...but in the end, the call of adventure was too strong to ignore.

R.F. Maclay is the pen name of an outstanding graphic designer and advertising filmmaker. His international career began as an electrician's apprentice, but he quickly realized that he was destined to work creatively. His family and friends were skeptical at first...but now, 20 years later, the passionate, self-taught graphic designer and filmmaker has delighted record labels, brand-name products and tech companies with his work, as well as making a name for himself as a commercial filmmaker and illustrator. He's also a walking encyclopedia of film and television series.

www.RobertsMaclay.com

Printed in Great Britain
by Amazon